The Long Dark Night of
Baron Samedi

The Long Dark Night of Baron Samedi

JOHN WYLLIE

PUBLISHED FOR THE CRIME CLUB BY

DOUBLEDAY & COMPANY, INC.

GARDEN CITY, NEW YORK

1981

All of the characters in this book are fictitious, and any resemblance to actual persons, living or dead, is purely coincidental.

The quotations which head chapters two to eighteen, inclusive, are taken from an unpublished work on West Africa that is in the author's possession.

Library of Congress Cataloging in Publication Data

Wyllie, John, 1914-
   The long dark night of Baron Samedi.
   I. Title.
PR6073.Y58L6   1981   823'.914
ISBN: 0-385-17755-0   AACR2
Library of Congress Catalog Card Number 81-3229

The Long Dark Night of
Baron Samedi

CHAPTER 1

. . . the reek of fear and bewilderment . . .

The woman and the two men met as they had agreed they would on the beach outside the old barracoon.

It was 3 A.M. and a bright moon, sitting low on the horizon and just about to go off-shift, stretched their shadows across the sand beside them.

The only living creatures which were disturbed by their intrusion were a few horseshoe crabs exploring the high-water mark along the shore for offal. They were sinister-looking creatures because they were featureless, their sensory organs and legs concealed beneath a cube of shell. The one appendage visible was a long skeletal tail which they dragged along the sand behind them, making them look like mobile, inverted saucepans.

The woman and the two men were familiar with them and therefore they ignored them.

Presently, they entered the barracoon via the narrow port through which the slaves had once been dragged out onto the beach and down to the edge of the sea and the waiting canoes or long boats that would take them, shivering with fear, out to the brigs.

That port, in the building's thick walls, was the last sight of Africa that had been allowed to them before they were shipped, packed together as tightly as the closed fingers of a man's hand, to North America, the West Indies, or Brazil. Many of them died on the way and were thrown overboard as jetsam. Others sickened, and if the captain felt that their illness might infect the rest of the cargo, they too, alive or dead, were thrown overboard, because insurance was not paid for damaged goods, only for total loss.

Earlier along their road to slavery the natural terror the Africans had felt when they were torn by other Blacks from their homes was compounded by the belief that the white men to whom they were sold were cannibals. They expected that they were on their way to some kind of abattoir.

Of the three people who entered the barracoon, however, not even one noticed that, though the building was empty, the reek of fear, bewilderment and despair still lingered in every corner, left there by the men and women who, over a period of close to six hundred years, had passed through it. In fact, two of the visitors were actually bent on adding to the building's accumulation of ugly memories. They left a little before dawn, using the same port that they had used when they had entered.

The third visitor remained behind in the flesh if not in the spirit.

CHAPTER 2

CREDO   There is an accumulation of experience and consciousness
lodged with the ancestors. It is a storehouse in which the lasting
essence of all human beings is stored. Those who act as keepers
and dispensers of the wisdom held in that place hear all, see all
and judge men by what they see and hear in accordance with the
laws of nature which, to them, have stood immutable since time
began.

"*Il est mort,*" the brigadier told Dr. Quarshie.

It was a superfluous statement. The dead man's carotid artery
had been cut as neatly as it might have been had he been the victim of an experienced butcher.

He lay with his head at the top of a sloping stone slab, about
the height and size of an altar, which stood in the circular central
courtyard of the barracoon.

The man was fat and naked and his shining, black, pudgy face
was still adorned with a pair of rimless spectacles. A pool of
blood at the foot of the stone block indicated that he had died
where he lay.

The brigadier looked at Quarshie and respectfully waited for
the big man to make some comment. As NCO in charge of the
small detachment of police on the Île de Sintra, murder was not a
crime with which he was familiar. He was therefore delighted that
Quarshie happened to be holidaying at the hotel on the island and
he was also delighted that when he conveyed this information to
his superior in Gambion, a couple of miles away across the sea, he
had been told to request the Doctor's assistance at once.

The Doctor, on his part, had already formed a good opinion of
the brigadier because, in this unexpected emergency, he had acted
promptly and efficiently.

The murdered man had been discovered very early in the morning by an old crone who was paid to sweep out the courtyard, the

cells and the other rooms which surrounded it every day before the barracoon was opened to tourists.

She had roused the brigadier from his bed with the whites of her eyes showing around the irises and her nearly toothless jaws shaking as if she had the palsy.

The brigadier had immediately awakened the other four members of the squad, armed them, and posted two of them to cover both entrances to the barracoon, the one from the sea and the one to the village, to prohibit all access without his authorisation. He had then sent his other two men to prominent points around the island from which they could watch the beach and other landing places. He had also sent the town crier around the island to inform everyone that there was a ban on all people leaving the island, and that the gendarmes had orders to shoot anyone trying to get away.

It was after that that he had telephoned his superior in Gambion, had told him about the murder and that Quarshie and an Ebonese judge named Kwamé Oturu were staying at the hotel. His superior had returned his call very quickly and had told the brigadier that the Judge, though retired, would be appointed as *juge d'instruction* and that Quarshie should be asked to make an immediate assessment of the case under the Judge's supervision.

Since the Judge was Quarshie's friend and, in fact, the reason for his visit to the island, the Doctor had complied with this request though he had avoided committing himself beyond "making an immediate assessment." "After all," he had told the Judge, "I am a foreigner here on holiday."

Now Quarshie said, "There is no evidence of any struggle. So what does that suggest, my friend?"

"Perhaps, m'sieu, the man was *hors de combat* before the killer went for his knife?"

"Precisely." Quarshie looked around and then, indicating some wooden benches, he said, "If we put three of those together we can lift the man's body onto them so that I can examine him. We can, then, look more carefully at the flogging block, for that is what this thing is, isn't it?"

"It is, m'sieu. You see the rings on the sides? They were used to secure a man's arms and legs before he was subjected to his punishment."

As they moved the benches Quarshie asked, "Do we know who the man is, brigadier?"

"Yes, m'sieu. An important man; the head of GES, *les Gardiens de l'État Souverain,* Monsieur Darapa's personal police."

"Personal police? Or secret police?"

The brigadier shrugged. "Here we speak of personal police, m'sieu."

Though the brigadier almost matched Quarshie in size and strength the two men found it difficult to move the body. Had rigor mortis been complete it might have been easier. As it was, the corpse was a sodden and slippery weight. Also they were distracted by the fact that as they moved the man they found that his body had been concealing an intricate pattern drawn on what had been the whitewashed stone with some kind of black powder.

When they had carefully laid their burden on the benches they went back to examine the markings.

After a moment Quarshie said, "I used to see things like this when I was a very young man at the meetings of the vudu cult near my home. This drawing is called a vevé. It is a diagram which the priests make to explain to their people what the loa, the gods, have told them to do. But, since they are all drawn in a secret code, only those who have been initiated into the specific cult would understand what they are all about. We must have a careful copy made of this one and see what, if anything, it tells us. For the moment I think we shall learn more from the body."

He turned back to the dead man and started his examination.

As he worked he voiced his findings so that his companion would understand what he was doing.

He said, "No sign of contusions or injury to the head though the fact that I had difficulty closing the man's eyelids suggests that rigor mortis is beginning to set in. That might mean that he has been dead for upwards of about two hours. Rigor mortis usually starts with the face muscles." And he continued explaining his actions as he worked down the man's body. They turned him over and the Doctor continued with his work without comment until he reached the backs of the man's legs. There, as he examined the skin minutely, he pointed to a mark on the femoral artery and a slight swelling. "The skin was punctured here. I think this may suggest the method used by the murderer. It will also confirm the observation you made that the dead man was *hors de combat* before he was killed. One could develop a theory based on these findings which would also explain why the body was unclothed. However, we, or someone else, will need to go much further with the investigation before arriving at any final decision. Even here, in the barracoon, there is much more work to be done and the sooner we get on with it the better. It would be wise, my friend, to arrange for the body to be sent to the pathology lab at the University College hospital. I know Dr. Pierre Marchais there. He should be asked to perform the autopsy."

*

When the man had left him, Quarshie, alone in the barracoon, which was still guarded by the two policemen, sat down to review the situation.

Though it was only a little after eight o'clock the day was already beginning to heat up and Quarshie chose to settle himself on a bench in the shade.

He and his wife had been invited by the Judge to spend a few weeks as his guests at the Hôtel de la Plage, because the old man was writing a book on slavery and he wanted Quarshie to provide him with a medical viewpoint on some of the evidence he had and also to help with the authorities he was using whose work was in English. Quarshie, because he had taken his medical degree at McGill University in Canada, was fluently bilingual in French and English; whereas the Judge's English was no better, he claimed, than workaday, though he spoke Portuguese, German, and French. It was on the strength of his linguistic capabilities, as well as his legal training, that he had spent several years as one of the jurors at the International Court in The Hague.

The old man had chosen to work on his book on the Île de Sintra because his brother owned and managed the Hôtel de la Plage and because of the island's long association with slavery. As early as 1462 the Portuguese had first settled there and had started to develop the place as a slaving depot. It is a kidney-shaped island a little over a mile long and about a half a mile wide. By comparison with the mainland the Portuguese had found the place relatively cool and free from the miasma that, in their belief, caused the fever which was then not yet known as malaria.

Nowhere on the island was it possible to be out of earshot of the sound of the sea as it washed over the surrounding rocks.

The island supported two or three hundred natives, mostly connected with fishing or tourism.

Since it was located only a few degrees north of the equator the force of the sun was as fierce as the heat a blacksmith gets out of his forge as he pumps up his furnace to soften a piece of steel. However, the island is cooled a bit by the land and sea breezes and the frequently stormy winds which blew in off the South Atlantic. The winds were a feature for which most of the Gambionaises were profoundly grateful. Only the palm trees seemed to resent the wind because it tore at them ceaselessly and left them bowed and ragged.

The sun and wind were responsible for another very visible feature of the scenery. Together they ravaged the colour wash and the plaster which were commonly used to dress the outside of the concrete-block or mud houses. In no more than a few weeks the colours became faded and the prying fingers of the wind and, in the season of storms, the rain, seeped through cracks and tore the plaster away leaving great flayed patches that revealed the basic materials underneath. It was an affliction which Quarshie had described to his wife as an acute case of actinic dermatitis.

The general atmosphere on the island was not one that Quarshie found salubrious. The aura left behind by the hundreds of years of human torture and degradation and the passage of perhaps two or three million souls through the very building he was sitting in had soured the island itself.

Quarshie decided he did not want to stay there. It was a bloody place, and its associations were all with brutality and human rapacity—a condition which had changed very little as the body of the man lying out in the courtyard testified and as Darapa's rule of the Ebony Coast also testified.

It seemed, he thought bitterly, as if the only thing men could be relied upon to do was to destroy each other, as the chief of the GES, the chief of an institution which used fear and torture to establish its power and make a profit from other men, had been destroyed.

No, he decided, he was not really concerned with solving the crime which had been committed in the barracoon. He had better things to do. Out of friendship for the Judge he would complete his initial assignment to make a preliminary investigation of the man's death, then he would turn over his findings to the Judge and remove himself and Mrs. Quarshie back to Akhana where he could find a little satisfaction from his work in his clinic and his encouragement and guidance of his adopted son.

With a sigh he got up and started a slow methodical search of the barracoon.

*

The morning sunlight in the courtyard of the slave house splintered the colours into the kind of mosaic one would see if one looked through a kaleidoscope with the patterns made up of shattered fragments of white, terracotta, yellow and black. In some cases, where the shadows fell on the colours, it gave them softer tones. The white belonged to the whitewashed walls, the terracotta to the soil and parts of the building that were adobe and had not been whitewashed, the yellow came from the sand on the floor and the black from the corners which gave shelter to the deepest shadows.

Quarshie stood in an arcade which fronted one half of the semicircle of cells that had once been used to contain slaves awaiting shipment. Above him there was a second floor identical to the one beneath it. In its simplest form the barracoon could be said to be built in the shape of a horseshoe. Fronting the sea there would have been the open end had this not been closed off to provide accommodation for the white trader and his guards. The other doorway was located at the crown of the horseshoe's arch.

On the inside the tunnel, which led to the doorway onto the shore, was flanked on each side by curving flights of steps to the first floor. In both this tunnel and the one which led to the door out to the village the walls were plastered with neatly hand-lettered statements about the slave trade. They were intended to be read by tourists.

"In 1500 our country was yielding 3,500 slaves and more a year to the Portuguese," read one of these signs.

"In 1561 the Queen of England invested £1000 in the slave trade and her profits exceeded 60 percent," read another.

"In 1592 the King of Spain issued a licence to his traders which allowed them to ship an annual quota of 38,250 slaves."

"By the end of the eighteenth century the European countries engaged in the slave trade included Britain, France, Spain, Holland, Denmark, Portugal, Sweden and Prussia. These countries were, later, joined by America."

"In ten years slavers from one city in England, Liverpool, shipped over 303,000 slaves.

"Says one historian, 'So far as the Atlantic slave trade is concerned, it appears reasonable to suggest that in one way or another, before and after embarkation, it cost Africa at least *fifty million souls*. This estimate . . . is certainly on the low side.'"

As he read these statements and others like them Quarshie tried to fight off the feeling of gloom they induced in him.

He turned away from the dismal records on the walls and the body of the dead man, still wearing his gold-rimmed glasses, caught his eye and dragged his attention back to the present.

Who was it had said, he wondered, "The world is a comedy to those that think, a tragedy to those that feel"? The memory of the quotation was followed by the thought that perhaps the man's death in this location was intended to have some sort of symbolic significance. He had better carry out his search of the building, he decided. He knew that he was faced with a subtle killer who had worked in such cold blood that he could plan to commit murder with the care and precision with which an engineer might plan an intricate piece of machinery.

Almost immediately his search turned up evidence which had been left so clearly in full view that it seemed as if he had been meant to find it.

A swift look around told him that cell after cell and room after room in the trader's quarters had nothing to offer. Not even the old crone who did the cleaning had disturbed the dust in them and all except one were empty.

In the exception a wide, thick sleeping mat lay on the floor. On it, set out as they would have been for a military inspection in a barracks, were what he assumed to be the dead man's clothes. A cream tussore suit, a pale blue poplin shirt, silk socks, fine cotton underwear and a pair of expensive brown shoes. The clothes were all neatly folded and set in a pile. There were no traces of blood anywhere.

A search of the pockets revealed a bunch of keys, some small change, a handkerchief, a black wallet containing a fold of paper money, a driving licence in the name of Kofi Akasaydoo, a doctor's prescription and half the stub of a ticket to the Pam Pam cinema in Gambion. The man had also been carrying a pocket calculator and some carefully made notes on a piece of paper about a mineral called corundum.

It was a collection of items which told him very little. One final item, in which Quarshie took great interest, was a small wad of face tissues which had lipstick on it and was stained in other ways. It had been tucked under the mat.

At that moment the brigadier came back with two of the stewards from the hotel, who carried a sheet and stretcher.

One of them whistled softly when he saw the dead man. Then they covered the body with the sheet and with a struggle got the corpse onto the stretcher. The brigadier said, "I have made arrangements about the post-mortem, m'sieu. They are sending a police launch for the late Monsieur Akasaydoo. They are also sending me some reinforcements. Is there anything else I can do?"

Quarshie gravely shook his head. "To be honest I don't know that there is anything anyone can do for the moment except to put these tissues in an envelope and send them with the body for analysis by Dr. Marchais. Then before you or I initiate any further action of any sort I must talk with my old friend the Judge, because obviously one's first suspicion must be that the crime was inspired by political motives. Wouldn't you agree?"

"But yes, m'sieu, certainly." The last word was spoken with great conviction.

Quarshie led the way back to the hotel where he was, himself, almost immediately put under arrest.

The stretcher rested on the casing over the engine and the chief of the GES men stood forward beside the helmsman.

Looking at the pale soles of the dead man's feet Quarshie thought of the standard attitude amongst illiterate Africans that there is no such thing as a natural death except amongst those who are very ancient. As the saying goes, "An enemy hath done this thing." In Akasaydoo's case there was no doubt about the truth of that statement. The problem was to identify which of the perhaps hundreds of the man's enemies had been cool and capable enough to murder him. Anyway, he thought, it was not going to be his concern. After he had found out what Darapa wanted—and it could not, he thought, be anything very serious—he and Mrs. Quarshie would pack their bags and go home.

"Why does the President want to see me?" he asked one of the men beside him.

The man was less brutal in his manner than his leader.

"He does not tell us, m'sieu, why he does things, or why we should do the things he tells us to do."

"You are trained killers, aren't you?"

The man shrugged. "Some men are trained to sentence men to death. Others are trained to fight, kill or die for their country. We are of those people."

A simple way, Quarshie thought, to rationalise murder.

*

In a little over ten minutes the launch docked just astern of an enormous Russian fish-factory ship. There was a closed truck there for the corpse and a big, black Mercedes for the GES men and Quarshie.

Clearly the driver was not concerned about the impression his route through the town made on his passengers. Had he been he would probably have taken the Corniche road, which follows the coast up from the docks to the centre of the city. He took, in fact, the most direct route, which passes through a couple of miles of *bidonvilles,* slums. In the past, when most of the fuel used for lights was kerosene, it had usually been delivered in tin four-gallon cans. The metal could easily be manipulated to provide a plating over roofs or the sides of shacks, which were usually made of mud or any rough dunnage the builders could salvage from the docks. *Bidon* in French means tin can, so slums became tin-can towns.

In Gambion the *bidonvilles* have open drains and no sewerage system. Water is supplied only to stand-pipes. These conditions are in stark contrast with the other part of the town, on the hill, with its high-rise office-blocks, apartments and hotels where, of course, there is underground sewerage, water piped to every room where it is needed, as well as every other form of comfort.

It was worth recognising, Quarshie thought, that the crime rate in the westernised part of the town was four times greater than it was in the *bidonvilles*. There was more display of wealth there and therefore more to steal and to kill for.

Just before reaching the downtown area the car passed through a section known as *Larronnesseville*, "the town of women robbers." In fact it is the red-light district, which advertises itself by its curtained doorways. The curtains are drawn if the woman in the hut has a customer, open if she is available.

Driving along Avenue de Gaulle, a wide divided highway with trees down the centre of it and on each side, they passed the market which was famous, or amongst most Africans infamous, for the fact that the market stalls were tenanted by white women who sold against the black. Generally the Whites traded in high profit items like meat and imported fruit and vegetables while the Blacks were left with local produce in which there was much less money.

Quarshie loathed Gambion, had loathed it when he was young before independence when there were only five thousand Whites there. Now that the Ebony Coast had become, nominally, a capital state in its own right and there were fifty thousand Whites there, he saw the whole place as a monstrous example of hypocrisy, with the man he was on the way to see on the top of the heap, where he was kept in place by French investment, French military power and French advisors.

Their destination was the Grand Palais, the President's residence. Once, when the city had been the capital of the whole of French West Africa, an area that has now been split into ten different countries and covers over two million square miles, it had boasted a Governor General who had ruled not only over vast territories but had the power of life and death over some twenty million people. So it had been seen to be fitting and right, then, that this residence should be built to impress His Excellency's true rank, nobility and power on his humble black subjects.

It had also been seen by Darapa to be fitting and right that he, while inheriting somewhat less power and rank and none of the nobility, since he had started his career as a messenger boy in a colonial government office, should inherit the Palais.

Another tradition he maintained was the ornamental military guard which were on duty at the Palais's gates. In their thigh-length boots, pants with a wide yellow stripe down the seams, scarlet, epauletted jackets, plumed and polished metal helmets and great curved sabres which they shouldered all the time they were on duty, they were more truly "chocolate soldiers" than anything which ever appeared in a Viennese operetta.

Quarshie had nothing but contempt for this neo-colonial display and was even more incensed against the ex-colonial power which encouraged such fantasies.

Darapa was as shrewd a politician and business man as any of the Frenchmen he had to deal with. Where Darapa exceeded the skill of his white advisors was in his ruthless pursuit of wealth and the power to, quite literally, get away with murder. The French in return for profitable concessions helped with the provision of funds, at the same time politely ignoring the way Darapa used them.

The building, when they reached it, was a very handsome one unlike the modern ones which were designed for other West African dictators. It was a relic of the colonial days built in the Moorish tradition, cool, extravagantly tiled and recklessly carpeted, not for beauty's sake but to deaden the echoes, now that even messenger boys wore shoes.

Quarshie was marched briskly along several corridors and up two flights of stairs—obviously the elevators were not for the use of police and their prisoners—until they came to a corridor where he was told to sit on a *fauteuil* between two of his armed guards.

The third man then disappeared through tall doors and remained out of sight for almost an hour. Others came and went through the same set of doors—some of them obviously flunkeys, some with white skins and one or two Africans whose air of dignity was somewhat soiled by the appearance, which can never quite be concealed, of men seeking favours.

In a most un-African way the corridor was without the sound of laughter or of voices raised in animated discussion.

Finally the leader of the GES men returned and jerked his head at Quarshie to indicate that he was to accompany him.

The man then led the Doctor, without his other escorts, through an anteroom where most of those Quarshie had seen pass through the tall doors were seated.

The next room contained two female typists, one of them a European woman, and a young male Black who was dressed in the elegant style of Paris. He was slender, languid and pretentiously well-mannered. He greeted Quarshie as an equal saying, "My dear doctor. It is an honour to meet you." And telling the GES man, as if he were a servant, "You can go, now, Emile."

Turning back to Quarshie he said, "The President is eager to see you. When I showed him his appointment book this morning he put his finger on your name and said, 'That encounter will be the highlight of my morning.' Will you follow me please, m'sieu."

With a practiced motion the man threw open double doors onto an enormous room furnished sparingly in the neo-classical style of the late eighteenth century in France.

The man who came round from behind his desk to greet the Doctor was of below average height and beginning to be stooped with age. He had a high forehead and eyes that were shrewd, humorous and predatory. Beneath a broad flat nose his flesh hung in a bulging flap over a mouthful of teeth and ended in lips which were unusually thin. Darapa's chin was his least conspicuous feature.

In a well-modulated voice he said, as he offered Quarshie his hand, "I am sorry to have subjected you to the manner in which you were conveyed to the palace. You were brought here in that way because those in charge don't know of any other method of carrying out my orders. One trains one's guard dogs to be fierce and it is then hard for them to behave otherwise. Please sit down." Darapa continued, "You are looking at my *bureau ministre* . . . I hope with approval. It came from the Palais Bourbon and was a gift from a gentleman of great influence in France. Perhaps you know him, Monsieur LeBoeuf."

"I have met him, *Monsieur le Président*. And it is a very impressive desk." Quarshie's one experience with LeBeouf had been when the man had tried his best to humiliate him.

"Ah, so you speak very good French, Doctor. I had been led to expect that you might speak our beautiful language in the atrocious accents of Quebec."

Darapa, sensing Quarshie's distaste for small talk, said, after a slight pause, "You will have realised, Doctor, that the death of the man Akasaydoo represents something more than common murder.

In most cases it is not very difficult to discover a motive. Usually there are a limited number of alternatives. However, I don't have to tell you that in this case there are as many reasons for killing the man as there are prisoners whom he has put behind bars."

"Or women who have been left widows by his actions, or men who have lost a brother. The Goloff still keep to the old laws of tribal revenge, I believe?" Quarshie suggested.

"You are right, Doctor. Now, since Akasaydoo was one of my representatives, you will understand that, in the first place, I would like to know who had such a serious grudge against him that he could make a ceremonial example of him. Second, I would like to be quite sure that when you find the answer it remains a fact which goes no further than Judge Oturu and myself. Will you kindly give me that undertaking?"

Quarshie looked steadily at Darapa for several seconds while the President returned his stare just as steadily.

Finally he said, "I have not yet said, sir, that I will undertake the investigation. It is not the kind of occupation that appeals to me."

"But we all have to do things sometimes that we don't like doing." The President's tone was conciliatory. "And you know I hold some cards with which I could very easily force your hand. When you left the Île de Sintra you were aware, I think, that your wife was under surveillance. Judge Oturu's family—he has two fine boys and a pretty daughter as well as his wife—are also being guarded against any possible attack"—Darapa paused significantly —"by the wrong people. That is, people whom I don't command. When you have carried out what you have to do then you and your charming wife will, of course, be free to return home and the Judge will be happily reunited with his family."

The threats were given in a matter-of-fact tone of voice and with a smile twitching at the corners of Darapa's wide mouth.

"I would like to speak with Colonel Jedawi to . . . to clear my . . ."

The President interrupted Quarshie.

"That will not be necessary, Doctor. I have already spoken with him. Your President wanted a *quid pro quo,* of course, for your services and I was glad to concede it."

"May I know what it is?"

"You will remember that we caught some of your countrymen smuggling a truckload of cocoa out of our country last month.

The penalty by law on our side of the border is harsh. Smuggling is a wicked occupation. On condition that you stay and work for us I have undertaken to hand the men over to your people for prosecution by your authorities, whose judgements in such cases are somewhat less extreme than ours. So your work for me will be buying the lives of some of your own people. That is, of course, if you are successful."

Controlling an instinct to take the little man opposite him by the throat, Quarshie nodded. He did not trust himself to speak.

"Then, Doctor, you are free to go, unescorted, though somebody will be keeping you in sight. Oh, and by the way, the brigadier on your island, who has a good record with the police, has been instructed to help you in every way he can."

The President got up to indicate the end of the meeting but Quarshie remained seated. He said, "You are overlooking something, sir. If I am to be successful, I have to start at the beginning."

"Oh?"

"You say the man worked for you so you must know a lot about him. I would like to ask you some questions. Also, Akasaydoo must have had an office and a residence here in Gambion. I would like your authority to search them both."

Darapa sat down again. After a thoughtful pause he said, "Of course, you are right, Doctor, but I have no time to answer your questions now. However, I can offer you a substitute who knows as much about Akasaydoo as I do. She will also accompany you when you search the man's apartment and his office. She is my confidential secretary, Madame de Gobineau."

The name was familiar to Quarshie but he could not think why.

Darapa flicked the switch on his intercom set and said, "Natalie, would you come in here, please?"

As Quarshie had expected, the President's confidential secretary was the white woman he had seen outside.

When she came in Quarshie stood up.

She was solidly built and Quarshie guessed that she was in her late thirties. Plainly dressed in green cotton frock she wore only one piece of jewellery, apart from a wedding ring, and very little make-up. The jewellery was a simple gold chain with a reproduction of an *Akua'ba* doll as a pendant. The doll is normally used by Ashanti girls as a charm to ensure that they bear beautiful children.

"Natalie, as you know, this is Dr. Quarshie who is going to be investigating Akasaydoo's death. He asked me to answer some questions about Akasaydoo and also for permission to search his office and his apartment. You know as much, if not more, than I do about the dead man and I would like you to answer the Doctor's questions and accompany him both to the apartment and to the office to ensure that he gets all the . . . co-operation he needs." Quarshie wondered if he had been right to think that the President had made a deliberate and meaningful pause before the word "cooperation." Was the President saying, in fact, that Natalie should see to it that he did not poke his nose into files and details that should not be his business?

Madame de Gobineau inclined her head slightly towards Quarshie to acknowledge the introduction but did not offer to shake hands.

She said, "Pleased to meet you, sir. My English is not so very good."

Darapa laughed and told her, "Then if you get into difficulties, Natalie, you can speak French, because the Doctor speaks our language with great elegance."

"My language, madame, is Miwi, but I have both English and French as equal second languages."

"Ah," said the President, "a believer in *négritude,* a man after my own heart."

They descended to the ground floor in an elevator.

It had been Madame de Gobineau's suggestion that they go to her house to talk because there they would not be interrupted.

Her attitude towards Quarshie was cool and correct. She treated him as she would have treated a visiting foreign diplomat. It was an exercise in which, he felt sure, she had had a lot of experience. She had done her homework, too, because as she drove, and she drove very well, she questioned him about some of his earlier cases. When he commented on her knowledge she admitted she had had his file sent over from the office of the *Directeur de la Sûreté* and had been studying it. "It is my job to know as much as I can about the people who have dealings with the President."

"I find it surprising that the file the *Sûreté* keeps on me is as comprehensive as your comments suggest."

Quarshie, watching his companion's profile, thought he detected a faint smile as she replied, "The file is really the responsibility of Monsieur LeBoeuf's department. It seems you outwitted him once and anyone who can do that gains a lot of respect in that Monsieur's eyes."

"But not enmity, madame?"

Madame de Gobineau did not answer him directly. She said, "I don't think, m'sieu, from what I have read of you, that it is going to help either of us if we spar with each other. It will be a waste of time. It is my business to make sure that what you learn about the dead man is precisely what you need to know to help you find the murderer. It does not go one iota beyond that. *Entendu?*"

"*Entendu,* madame." Quarshie agreed with a smile.

Quarshie noted that they were heading towards one of the more exclusive parts of the city on the opposite side of Gambion to Larronnesseville. Eventually they turned onto the northern section of the Corniche, an area known amongst the Africans as the "white ghetto."

"Why is the President so eager for me to undertake this investigation? Surely it is a GES problem and one they should solve."

"Most of the men in the GES are not very intelligent, m'sieu. They are chosen because of that fact. Blind obedience is what is called for and it is not a characteristic which appeals to men of intelligence. Besides, you are—how shall I put it—uncontaminated by factional loyalties or disputes. You can be expected to base your judgements on facts, not on feelings, no?"

The house was a rambling, old-fashioned bungalow in the colonial style, built around an open courtyard with flowers and a fountain in it. Across the back was the kitchen, pantry and storage space. Across the front, with a verandah on each side, were a large *salon* and dining room. On each side there were four bedrooms with verandahs only onto the courtyard. They all had bathrooms *en suite.*

"My husband, he is the chief advisor on police matters here, is away on tour up in the north."

"And you have no children, madame?"

"I have two, Doctor. They were both born here in Gambion but they are away at school in France."

She opened a screen door onto the verandah which looked out across the road to a narrow stretch of grass, the cliffs and the sea.

"Sit down, m'sieu. I will have the boy bring you some beer. That is the correct drink, is it not? I will be back in a moment."

Quarshie leant back in a comfortable chair and closed his eyes. There was a lot to think about. De Gobineau; the details he had been looking for came back. Count Joseph de Gobineau had been the author of a tract which had had an important impact on the people of the French Second Empire. It was a treatise called "An Essay on the Inequality of the Human Races," and it had advanced an early form of the theory that the Aryan races of the world were inherently superior. As a fact, at the moment, it was a little cloud floating in an otherwise empty sky casting an insubstantial shadow. It might have more meaning later.

Madame de Gobineau's position as Darapa's confidential secretary had more immediate significance, especially since her husband's position was probably one of the most important in the country. The man's powers might even exceed those of the President himself.

In the past in West Africa, in many large tribes, secret societies worked with the central government to share the responsibility for administration, supervision and adjudication in economic life, education, sexual conduct, medical services and even organised entertainment and recreation. The Poro society, for instance, held power amongst the Mende, one of the largest and historically most important tribes, for well over four hundred years. *"Plus ça change, plus c'est la même chose."* Today, it was the secret police rather than the secret societies who held the power. So Darapa and the French were only subscribing to a system which had proved itself over hundreds of years.

The servant brought Quarshie a couple of litre bottles of beer, a bottle opener and a glass.

"That suffices, m'sieu?" he asked.

Quarshie nodded.

Madame de Gobineau returned. She had obviously taken a quick shower because her hair was wet and she had changed her plain "business" dress to something a little more chic and feminine. It was largely transparent and showed that she was wearing a very lacy slip underneath it.

Quarshie had again risen to his feet as she reappeared and as they sat down he said, "So you knew Monsieur Akasaydoo quite well?"

"I knew his reputation and what was in his dossier. I also met him from time to time when he came to see the President or at meetings of those officials who were involved in national security."

"What did you think of him as a man?"

Madame de Gobineau shrugged. "He was not, I think, a person

whom anyone would choose as a friend but one of whom it would be better not to make an enemy."

"Why?"

"He had a *penchant* for constructing plots. In them he assigned people roles and motives which had to fit *his* ideas."

She clapped her hands and called for the boy. When he came she told him, "Bring master some nuts and fetch me a gin and tonic."

"How did the President regard him?"

"His Excellency seems to have lost some of the regard he used to have for him. Akasaydoo bungled one or two assignments and got some unwelcome publicity. Clandestine operations are not much use to anyone unless they remain clandestine."

"So why did he not get rid of him?"

"M'sieu, you cannot be so naïve as to think that in the secret service one can hire and fire people as one might in a store or in a construction company. People on the inside know too much to be allowed to be left free to use it when and how they like. So the most sensible way is to eliminate them, or to have them eliminated."

It was said in the cold-blooded way someone might speak of chess pieces on a board.

"But presumably that was not what happened in this case or the President would not be asking me to try to find the murderer?"

Again Madame de Gobineau shrugged. "That would be the obvious assumption, m'sieu. The one I would subscribe to."

"And Akasaydoo's private life?"

"He kept it very well concealed. I shall be as interested as you are to see what we find, if anything, at his apartment."

"Do you know anything about any current operations in which he might have been employed?"

"As ever he was building up dossiers on people in public life and on some people whose lives were not so public."

"Can you give me any names?"

"No. I can only confirm or deny any evidence you may come across concerning such people. I might even have to warn you off some of them because their activities are unlikely to be of interest to you in your role as investigator into Akasaydoo's death. It will be better for you not to get involved with any activities that are not of practical interest to you. I am trying to protect you, you understand, from the kind of dangers which might not be clear to you. You are, in many people's opinions, an unusual and valuable man and we would like to keep you alive."

"I am grateful for your consideration, madame."

The two bottles of beer stood empty on the side-table by the arm of Quarshie's chair.

"Would you like some more beer? Or shall we go and look at Aka's apartment?"

"The latter, please, madame."

Akasaydoo had lived in a penthouse apartment in one of the new high-rise blocks in downtown Gambion.

It would have been impressive had not someone with destructive instincts visited the place ahead of Madame de Gobineau and Quarshie.

All the drawers in all the *commodes* had been opened and their contents dumped on the floor, the padding on all the *fauteuils* and the mattresses on the beds had been ripped, the backs had been torn off the pictures and some of the carpets had been half rolled up.

Quarshie said, "It would be nice to know what the people who did this were trying to find."

The moment they had entered the apartment he had glanced at Madame de Gobineau to see how she reacted. She appeared to be surprised.

"Perhaps, madame," he said, "you would be kind enough, while I look round, to ring up your friends amongst the police and others to find out whether this was their work, and if it was, what they hoped to discover."

"Certainly, Doctor."

Quarshie's search was slow and thorough. It turned up two minor items which interested him. In a pocket in the coat of a suit he discovered half a cloakroom ticket. Glancing through some of the books on a table in the bedroom, he discovered that though the covers suggested material about travel, Akasaydoo's real interests were not the contours of hills and mountains but the contours of female flesh, particularly views which proved his tastes to be both sadistic and perverted.

At Akasaydoo's office Quarshie made another discovery which, he felt, might or might not have relevance to his investigation.

It was a file in the IN basket on his desk which had a letter attached to the cover from a Dr. Nigel Sharp. Quarshie had met the man. He was staying at the Hôtel de la Plage, the only hotel on the Île de Sintra. He was a Jamaican and a professor of anthropology at a university in England.

The file indicated that there had been a comparatively short exchange of letters relating to some research work the professor had been carrying out on Ebony Coast families whose ancestors had been slaves. It appeared from the correspondence that the GES had become suspicious of Dr. Sharp's activities. They seemed to think that the professor had been asking questions which, Akasaydoo had noted, went beyond the limits of the subject of Sharp's research. In one letter Akasaydoo had written of a "sensitive issue" that Sharp had been investigating without specifying any further details.

Quarshie had asked Madame de Gobineau whether he might take the file away with him and she had shaken her head. "I would have to discuss that question with my husband," she told him. "Though I could permit you to make notes, if that would suffice. The correspondence seems harmless enough and Aka seems to have been taking no more than normal precautions. I will note the file number and report that its contents interested you to my husband." As an obvious afterthought she added, "And, of course, to the President."

When they parted Madame de Gobineau had told him that her enquiries had not produced any evidence that the raid on Aka's flat had been in any way officially inspired. Then she picked up the phone and ordered the police launch to take Quarshie to the island, wished him "good luck" and offered him her hand.

It was a gesture that Quarshie saw as a sign that he had passed a test and had won her approbation. He might even receive, he thought, a good report in the note she would add to the file which was kept by France's *émminence grise* in West Africa, Monsieur LeBoeuf.

CHAPTER 4

CREDO "There is nothing that there is not; whatever you have a word for, that is": so speaks the wisdom of the Yoruba priests. ". . . every human thought, once expressed, becomes reality. For the word holds the course of things in train and changes and transforms them. And since the word has this power, every word is an effective word, every word is binding. There is no 'harmless,' noncommittal word. Every word has consequences."

The Quarshies and the Judge were strolling slowly around the narrow, unpaved streets of the village on the island.

It was evening, the worst of the heat had been carried away by the regular shift of wind. The trio, all of whom had had an exhausting day, talked at random about the things which surfaced through the turmoil disturbing their minds.

They had just passed the entrance to the barracoon when Quarshie said, "There are plenty of Blacks still engaged, here, in selling their people into slavery, only now instead of physical slavery it is economic slavery. The Mercedes the politicians ride around in and their television sets are the equivalents of the guns and the gin of the old days."

The others greeted his statement with silence.

Presently they came to a piece of high ground from which they could see the major part of the island spread out below them.

At the centre of the huddle of huts and a few two-story houses was the Place de la Liberté. On one side of it was the hotel. On the other there were two shops which catered to tourists. Part of the third side was occupied by the *poste de police* and a small school. The final side was dominated by a building almost as imposing as the hotel. It was one of Darapa's holiday residences and the place where Akasaydoo had been staying when he had been killed.

These buildings flanked four sides of a square around one of the island's most unique features, an immense baobab tree. It was over thirty feet in diameter and with a little imagination it was easy for anyone looking at it to believe that it was a huge peg driven through the island to ensure that the Île de Sintra was not washed around the bay by the changing tides.

Not far from where they stood was a mini-mosque where several white-robed and white-bearded old gentlemen sat on a verandah in reflective silence. A little later, as the trio walked past them, one of these devotees of Islam said loudly enough for the Judge to hear and translate, "God is great and merciful. Yesterday, my wife bought six eggs in the market. They cost twice as much as they did this time last year. I do not know where it will end but we must have faith that it is His will and therefore that it is right." The solemnity with which the words were spoken brought a momentary smile to all their faces, and Quarshie said, "Things are tough all over."

Then, reverting to their own problems, Mrs. Quarshie said, "I don't know what right the man has to hold us here to do his dirty work against our will." She was talking of Darapa.

In his heavily accented English Judge Oturu told her, "I know, Prudence, it is most unjust and I feel myself responsible. Of course, if Quarshie was not so good at his job . . ." The Judge left the statement open-ended and went on to voice a different thought. "I have often wondered what makes a successful criminal investigator and I have come to the conclusion that he has to be a man who wants people to be good, even if he finds that most of them are bad. Unlike Quarshie, I would be hopeless because I would suspect everybody who even breathes the same air as the victim of having poisoned it."

Quarshie smiled and said, "You flatter me, Kwamé." Then solemnly he asked, "Could you bear to sit down here for a few moments and go over again the evidence that came to light while I was away?"

"Here" was a seat by the shore line where each breath of wind rattled the dead palm fronds over their heads and the screech of a sea-gull seemed to ricochet across the water towards the distant horizon. Near their feet the sea sucked noisily at the rocks.

The Judge frowned with concentration. "The brigadier found the knife that was probably used to commit the murder. It had just been thrown away along the high-water mark. Not even had the bloodstains been cleaned off it. It is the kind of thing you can buy at any tourist shop. A cheap piece of steel with an elaborate leather hilt and usually a leather *fourneau,* scabbard, no? It has been sent for tests.

"In a patch of very dry sand the brigadier is finding footprints but there was not very much he could tell from them because the wind has made them into holes without shape.

"The other important thing he has for you are the records of the people landing from or leaving on the ferries. The *agents de police* check everyone, because for some time people sneak ashore at night in canoes, with bottles of whiskey and gin off the ships. There is no *douane* at the point where they land from the ferry. The police don't take names from people here, but they are checking identity cards and passports. If any of the visitors seem exceptional they make note of them. I think those lists would be good for more looking, no? I will get them for you if you wish."

"Please do," Quarshie told him and then turned to his wife. "And you had a session with Professor Sharp, Prudence?"

"He came and sat at the table where I was drinking coffee. The GES men were in the corner watching me. I don't know what they thought about his visit."

"Did he give any reason for joining you?"

"He asked if I was the wife of the famous Dr. Quarshie and when I said I was he wanted to find out what I knew about Akasaydoo's death. Of course I knew very little."

"Then?"

"Then he just talked, mostly about himself. He is a professor of anthropology at some university in England."

"Did he say why he is here?"

"He is doing a research project into Goloff customs."

"Ah. This is not what his correspondence with Akasaydoo suggested. Did he say he knew the dead man?"

"Yes. He told me he did not like him, or trust him. He also told me that he does not sleep well and that he was sitting in the window of his room at the hotel, it faces onto the Place de la Liberté, and he saw Akasaydoo come out of the front door of Darapa's house about three o'clock in the morning. He said I should tell you. That is really why, I think, he wanted to talk to me."

"What did you think of him, as a man?"

Mrs. Quarshie considered the question for a moment and then she said, "I thought he was ever so nice."

Quarshie grinned at his wife's Englishism. She had a few of

them she had picked up from a nurse he had in the clinic who had done her training in England.

Quarshie turned back to the Judge. "Before all this happened, Kwamé," he said, "we were talking one day about your book on slavery and you said, I think, that there was a Haitian on the island. His name came up because you said the mix of tribes there is greater than anywhere else and that this had to do with the development of voodoo. I would like to consult him about the vevé symbol we found beneath the dead man."

"I will take you to him. His name is Anton Antibonite. Very strange man. I don't know what to make of him. He has been here long. Keeps himself to himself. He lives with a widow, sort of prostitute. More of a wife *provisoire,* temporary, than a prostitute. There are lot of women like that in the Zongos who give strangers all the comforts of home, cook for them, wash for them, keep house for them."

"And what is his background?"

"*Franchement,* I don't know. The GES must have a file on him. It's a mystery to me how he is getting a permit to stay here. He mentioned that he lived in Paris at some time and also in Malinkal. He is well-educated man but two times when I speak with him I am coming away with a feeling of *inquiétude.* There is something *fantasque* about him I can't identify. He has long, wild hair and a beard like the Rastafarians from Jamaica."

"Now tell me a bit about the politics here. You dropped a hint or two about your feelings; now I would like to have it all. Darapa is much too interested in the murder for there to be nothing political involved. What is your opinion?"

The Judge stared at the sea for a while. Some white tourists were skin-diving a little way out in the bay. Like everyone else on the island, they would be prohibited to leave or to go more than two or three hundred yards off shore. A police boat was keeping an eye on them.

The Judge made sure there was no one else within earshot before he said, "I hope that what I am going to tell you will never be repeated to anyone, under any circumstances. Even *sous serment* in a court of law. I am not trying to protect myself. I am old man so it does not matter what happens to me. I am thinking of my family. If I get myself in trouble again and Darapa choose to take his *rancune,* his hate, out against them it would be a terrible thing. You know he is already using this *menace* against me."

"Did he?" Quarshie asked.

"Yes. Once, ten years ago, because a judgement I gave displeased him, he sent me to a detention camp in the north and he limited the amount of money my wife can draw from the bank to just enough to keep her and the children alive. When relatives tried to help them the GES beat them."

"How terrible." Mrs. Quarshie shook her head unbelievingly.

"With Akasaydoo out of circulation there will certainly be a little less fear about the country. Quarshie, I will tell you in French, you can translate it for Prudence." When the old man had finished the Doctor told his wife, "Kwamé was talking of the American abolitionist called John Brown, a man who fought for an end to slavery. At one time he said, 'I, John Brown, am now quite certain that the crimes of this guilty land will never be purged away except by blood.' Kwamé said the same is true of this country and that what has happened here, to Akasaydoo, may be the beginning."

The Judge looked quizzically at Mrs. Quarshie. "Yes? You understand, Prudence? Many from the people who are working with the GES are men with criminal mentality but it is one that is twisted so that it is turning back on itself. At The Hague everyone called it the Gestapo mentality. It is a love of making people feel pain, *sadique.* I don't like it at all.

"In the case of Monsieur Akasaydoo," he continued, "it was a *chose,* a thing, of like father like son. Kofi's father serve the Whites, the French, in the same way the son served our President. Not that I think Darapa is bad all through. But, like the men he chose for the GES, he is thinking that there is such a thing as justifiable violence. Others, like me, would call it *inhumanité.* Law and order under his kind of *tyrannie* exists only for those people who think like he does. For people who have opinions of their own . . . well, they disappear, or they die. Monsieur Akasaydoo and his friends are our own type of Papa Doc's Tontons Macoutes. But here we have a difference. The French support Darapa, *ipso facto* they are supporting the GES. They even have white hoodlums who work for them. Is it enough for you to understand why you must never tell that I say to you all this?"

Quarshie shook his head sadly saying, "Of course we will say nothing, Kwamé. But is everything going well for Darapa?"

The Judge shrugged. "Rumours—there are always rumours—that Akasaydoo and Darapa have some kind of falling out." He sighed, *"Crimine ab uno disce omnes.* From a crime, one crime alone, you can know a nation. Here it is not a crime, but a criminal and he is the head of state. Akasaydoo is also a criminal so who knows what happens when one criminal is having problems with another? Who knows what can come of it?"

"Usually," Quarshie said, "the outcome is murder."

CHAPTER 5

CREDO The universe is based on two concepts. One relates to the belief that all matter vibrates. The other concerns the general movement of the universe as a whole. The original germ of life is symbolised by the smallest cultivated seed, called by the Dogon the *kize izi,* "the little thing." This seed, quickened by internal vibration, bursts the enveloping sheath and emerges to reach ultimately the uttermost confines of the universe.

At the same time the unfolding of all matter proceeds in a zigzag line around a slowly mounting spiral. The zigzag symbolises the perpetual alternation of opposites, right and left, high and low, odd and even, male and female, etc., and represents the principle of twin-ness, of pairs of opposites which support each other but must always be kept in equilibrium. In short, the order of the cosmos is observed and conceived by the Dogon as a projection, boundlessly expanded, of events and phenomena which occur in the infinitely small as well as in the unbounded universe.

Back at the hotel the receptionist told Quarshie, "Professor Marchais wants you to phone him. And, Doctor, I found this letter for you on the counter."

"You did not see anyone leave it there?"

"*Non,* m'sieu."

To the Judge Quarshie said, "That will be the report on the autopsy." As he spoke he tore open the envelope. It contained a brief note in English, badly written and atrociously spelt.

"Sir," it read, "I have to tell you their is a man on the Ile de Sintra wot is a very bad enimey of Akasaydoo. He has for his name Adedeni Sayonnbo. He is bornubian and was disgrased by Akasaydoo bekos he was kort smugling hash. He went to prison. He hayted Akasaydoo enuff to kill him. I know bekos that is wot he is telling me."

Quarshie handed the note to the Judge and after the old man had read it he said, "Someone paying off an old score, I think."

"You are not going to ignore it?"

"No. Certainly not. But neither am I going to say the problem is solved." And he asked the receptionist to call Professor Marchais.

When the call came through Quarshie made notes on a pad as he talked. At the end of five minutes he thanked the professor and hung up.

To the Judge and Mrs. Quarshie he said, "We'll go out on the terrace and have a beer while I look through all this information." The others watched him scan his notes. With his second beer he said, "Dr. Marchais is nothing if not thorough. I now know the condition of every organ in Akasaydoo's body. For instance, 'The prostate gland shows advanced nodular hyperplasia with a prominent middle lobe' and there is 'an over-plus of tophus in his tissues.' Also he had had trouble with his spleen which suggests that he probably at one time or another had had bilharzia. So, if someone had not killed him he could, physically, have had a somewhat unhappy future. However, what interests us is the way he died. As I suspected he could have been attacked by someone with a hypodermic syringe while, perhaps, he was proving his manhood with a woman. Residues on him and on the paper tissues that I found tucked under the mat prove that his companion was certainly female. The murderer could have sat on his legs while the woman held him tightly with her arms and an accomplice could have inserted a hypodermic needle into the femoral artery.

"The substance used to knock him out appears to have been tubocurarine, which could have made him helpless in under two minutes. Then, I suspect, he was moved down to the flogging block, tied there, and the killer cut his throat. Without any means of regulating his breath artificially the tubocurarine, a modern form of curare, could have killed him by itself, though I doubt that it did because the amount of blood Akasaydoo lost suggests that his heart was still working to the end. A very clear case, I think, of premeditated murder. That he was tempted to some curious sex games in the barracoon fits in with the literature I found in his apartment."

Quarshie picked up the letter and read it again, held it up to the light, examined the writing carefully and said, "I think someone is playing games."

"Why, Quarshie?"

He shook his head. "It seems contrived. 'He has for his name

Adedeni Sayonnbo' is gramatically a French construction. So if the writer is French why isn't he writing in French? And if he has learned to speak English well enough to express himself as fluently as he does, he should be able to spell simple words like 'because' and 'what.' So, as a document it may well be more interesting than it seems to be on the surface."

"Especially since Adedeni is here on the island and what the writer says about him is true." The Judge made the statement without looking at Quarshie.

"You know him?" The note of surprise in Quarshie's voice was clear.

"He is a protégé of mine. His father is what the English call a barrister and a diplomat. He was ambassador here a couple of years ago and Adé went to the university here."

"And the bit about hashish?"

"Is true. He was supposed to have been smuggling it. The case did not come before me. He was and is a hashish smoker I'm sure. And that is already a crime. But I always suspect the smuggling charge was made up to discredit his father. Darapa had been trying to buy oil from Bornubia and they were not selling. Also they are saying some rude words in the press about Darapa because he is allowing the South African plane to land here for petrol and for giving asylum to a man who was leading a rebellion against the Bornubian government. In response the press here is running big headlines that the Bornubian Embassy was used as a sanctuary for drug smuggling led by Adé. He is sent to prison and then directly, after only a week, expelled from the country."

"So what is he doing back here, now?"

"Darapa is making a *volte-face.* He is saying there has been a miscarriage of justice and he suggests that it is Akasaydoo's fault. Normally, Akasaydoo is accepting the blame because it is the sort of thing he is paid to do. But this time . . ."

"This time?"

"I don't know. It has not worked that way, I think. There is the talk I told you about, that there has been a falling out. The business of Adé's involvement with drug smuggling may be part of the problem. That's Adé sitting over there."

Quarshie turned to look across the terrace. Seated alone at a table near the balustrade, with the sea behind him just beginning to reflect the impending sunset, Quarshie saw a tall, studious-looking young man. He had a modified Afro and wore gold-rimmed spectacles. He was reading a thick, heavy book which, Quarshie assumed, was some kind of reference work.

"He is a brilliant student, that's why he is my protégé. He is taking law. Do you want to meet him?"

Quarshie shook his head. "Later. He can't go away. There is something else that needs to be done, first. I have to take a look at Darapa's house, here, where Akasaydoo was staying. Are there any staff, or other people there?"

"Ponongo. Albert, to his friends. He was Aka's assistant. And a girl. I think I have heard her called Yasin."

"Do you know anything about either of them?"

"Ponongo has white blood. He might be the result of a union between a European and a Peule. You call them Fulanis, Prudence. He has a narrower face than most of us. Trained in Paris. Very quiet and, I think, intelligent. About the girl I know nothing. I think she is somebody's girl-friend. She's not one of our people—she could be a northerner, perhaps a Malinke. She is very beautiful. I would say that she would be better for Albert Ponongo than for Aka because, though the dead man had a lot of *ruse,* cunning, he had not, I think, much education, or inclination towards the things of the mind."

"Ponongo has that inclination?"

"I think so."

"Good. Let's go and have a look at them and at the house."

*

The door, with its ornate wrought-iron grille over the glass, was opened by a slender young man with a gold chain around his right wrist. From the lightness of his skin Quarshie assumed that he was Ponongo.

He acknowledged them with a slight nod of his head. "Doctor and Mrs. Quarshie," he said, holding out his hand to each of them in turn. "I was expecting you. You, too, sir." He bowed slightly to the Judge. "You will want to examine the house, no doubt. We have not touched anything since we heard of Monsieur Akasaydoo's murder. I am glad you were here, Doctor."

It was all said very deferentially and a little self-consciously because Mrs. Quarshie's gaze was fixed on him and her appraisal was as cool as he endeavoured to make his attitude. Indeed, her attention was so firmly on him that she failed to notice the girl who was standing behind him in the darker recesses of the hall-way.

Then Ponongo turned towards her, as she came forward to greet them. "This is Mademoiselle Yasin Barafat. A friend of mine and of Monsieur Akasaydoo."

Except for the difference in the skin colour they might, Quarshie thought, have been brother and sister. They had almost the same features and certainly the same elegance.

Yasin Barafat, Quarshie guessed, would be about twenty-four or five. She had her hair plaited in tiny pigtails that covered her head as if they had been woven together with over-sized knitting needles. She had a long graceful neck which matched an equally long graceful figure and her hands were as delicate and shapely as Mrs. Quarshie's.

Her voice was so soft that Quarshie had to bend towards her to hear the words as she said, *"Enchanté, madame et messieurs."*

Quarshie explained that his wife did not speak French and asked if their two new acquaintances spoke English, to which Ponongo nodded and the girl said, "Not ver' good, I am afraid, but maybe enough."

Looking at them both Mrs. Quarshie thought of Quarshie's theory of how the murder could have been carried out, and she wondered if the pair who had greeted them could have co-operated in undertaking an act of that nature. The girl hardly looked strong enough but slender people could, she told herself, in desperation exert quite remarkable strength.

Quarshie was saying, "Perhaps we shall get through this process most quickly if we could do the talking first. After that I would like to look around the house."

"Certainly, m'sieu."

"Good. Then perhaps we might go to whatever room Monsieur Akasaydoo was using as his office and I would be grateful if I could interview each of you separately."

"Of course. Then Yasin and I can contradict each other without embarrassment." Ponongo smiled as he said the words.

Quarshie returned the smile, "Exactly. Of course, m'sieu, you are used to interrogation procedures."

"I have attended a few, *Docteur*. Akasaydoo's room is here on the *rez de chaussée*. Yasin, perhaps you would entertain Mrs. Quarshie in the *salon*."

The suggestion fitted well with Quarshie's wishes because it would give his shrewd partner an opportunity to assess the personality of the young woman whose beauty he found more than somewhat disarming.

Quarshie waved the Judge in front of him as they followed Ponongo down the wide hallway to the back of the building where there was a room almost as splendid as the one in which Darapa had interviewed Quarshie earlier in the day.

There were brocade curtains and wall hangings. There was a lot of furniture with rococo curves and ormolu decorations. As might be expected in the tropical heat, high humidity and salt-laden atmosphere, most of the pieces were showing signs of deterioration that had little to do with their age.

Ponongo suggested that Quarshie sit down but the big man refused, not wanting to trust his weight to such fragile furniture.

He stood in the tall embrasured window with his back to the twilight in which the distant town was beginning to twinkle, as if with rhinestone brilliants, as the lights came on.

The Judge lowered himself gingerly into a chair while Ponongo, facing Quarshie, perched on a desk with peeling green leather in the centre and brass strips of ornamentation around the edge.

Quarshie's bulk loomed large and almost menacing in the window as he said, "You will forgive me if some of my questions are rather personal." And when Ponongo nodded he continued, "How long have you known the dead man?"

"About four years."

"He recruited you, personally?"

"No. The President put me in the position I hold."

"So you reported to him directly?"

"No, or rather, only with Monsieur Akasaydoo's permission."

"Never otherwise?"

"Well, if the President asked me a question over the phone or when Akasaydoo was not present of course I had to answer without consulting my *patron.*"

"You did your training in France?"

"Yes. After I took my *bac* I joined the military and was posted to a special group in the army. We were trained to deal with counter-insurgency and with urban guerrillas."

"Had Akasaydoo ever had any training like that?"

"When he did his training words like counter-insurgency and urban guerrillas were not known."

"But it was the kind of work he did?"

"Him and his father before him."

"Secret police?"

Ponongo shrugged. "Different words mean different things to different people."

"What I mean is that his work, your work, could lead to your making many enemies?"

"It not only could, it has."

"Do you know if the dead man had any specific enemies who might have liked to see him dead?"

"Specific, no. Potential, yes."

"Who?"

"Doctor, a number of men died because of his activities, our activities, or were sent to camps out in the bush." Quite gently he said to the Judge, "It even happened to you, I think, sir."

The Judge nodded his white head.

"And many of their friends and families felt badly enough to want to take revenge. All of them must be considered as enemies. They could easily number in the hundreds."

"Are you going to take Akasaydoo's place now that he has gone?"

"That will depend on the President's decision, Doctor. If he offers me the job it will be hard for me to refuse."

"Did the President have any trouble with Akasaydoo?"

"The President is the man to answer that question, sir."

"Let me put it another way. You were his closest associate. Did Akasaydoo ever mention to you that there were any disagreements between the President and your *patron?*"

"I am sorry, Doctor, your questions suggest that you might be trying to implicate the President in Akasaydoo's death. The Judge here is witness to that fact."

Quarshie seemed to grow a lot larger as he moved towards the younger man. "No, my young friend, I am not trying to implicate anyone. I am trying to get to the truth. I am also, on behalf of the President, trying to determine whose testimony I can rely on and who is likely to be evasive. And if they are evasive what motive they may have. Would you like to repeat what you have just said in front of President Darapa?"

There was a moment's silence while the two men faced each other. Finally Ponongo said, "I am not trying to be evasive. There has been quite a lot of talk about disagreements between the President and Monsieur Akasaydoo. I am not aware whether there was any truth in those statements or not. Most people have disagreements with the President from time to time but they don't discuss them with other people."

"Have you ever had any disagreements with the President?"

"I have."

"Did you raise them with him?"

Ponongo shook his head.

The salon into which Yasin led Mrs. Quarshie was unlike anything the plump, matronly Akhanian had ever seen.

The ceiling was painted with pictures of voluptuous white women sitting on clouds surrounded by pink-bottomed babies with little grey wings sprouting out of their shoulder-blades. There were marble columns where no columns were needed and they were accompanied by the whole rigmarole of Second Empire French splendour which fitted about as well into Africa as the works of Boileau, Corneille and Racine fitted into the classrooms of African secondary schools where ardent young Frenchmen, during colonial days, used to hammer them furiously into their students.

Yasin saw the look of amazement on Mrs. Quarshie's face and told her, "It is all a great big piece of nonsense, no? Like a black woman who paint her face with white woman's *cosmétiques*. It is so *prétentieux* . . . when the French are in this place maybe it is OK. But this man who is living here now, the President . . . with him it is very bad. I think he is black Frenchman . . . bad, bad black Frenchman."

It was an explosion of feeling which surprised Mrs. Quarshie.

"If you feel like that why are you living here?" she asked.

"Ah. I open too big my mouth." The girl was silent thinking over her indiscretion.

Then she shrugged. "It is better I make it easy for you, I think. Already I have plant the seed and everybody will be thinking I am making a big *tracas* if I don't say the truth about everything and not just in little pieces."

Mrs. Quarshie, who was feeling a little out of her depth with this chic young woman in surroundings which were most unnatural to her, said, "I am sure that would be most sensible, Miss Barafat." It seemed a safe thing to say.

"*Bon.* We should, please, sit down."

And there followed a "piece of story telling," as Mrs. Quarshie called it when she repeated it to her husband, which took her breath away.

"She kept calling me *'maman,'*" Mrs. Quarshie said, "and she talked as if she could not stop all the words coming out. It was a torrent."

Yasin's story had started back in her childhood.

"She began her story by saying, 'I mus' 'ave tell to myself a douzain times zat some day I am goin' to keel dat man vit my own 'ands.'" Mrs. Quarshie's imitation of Yasin was intentionally comic and she filled herself with delight over it, laughing with Quarshie at it. Suddenly she became serious and said, "I don't know why I am laughing. My goodness, Quarshie, she might have held him with her own hands while somebody else killed him, and I might have been talking to a murderess." Sobered, she went on to recount the rest of what Yasin had told her.

The girl had been about ten years old, she had told Mrs. Quarshie, when she had had her first brush with Akasaydoo and the GES. There had been signs on the walls around Gambion, at that time, which said, *"Ecrasez les blancs."* And the French colonialist government had been very much on the look-out for revolutionaries and agitators. The Judge had been correct in identifying her nationality: Yasin's father came from Malinkal and he was a schoolteacher at a big secondary school called the *Lycée Capitaine Bouet-Guillaume 3*. (Mrs. Quarshie's memory, like that of many African women, was astonishingly accurate.) At the same time the *Rassemblement Démocratique Africain* was a banned organisation and Darapa and Akasaydoo were already working for the French.

Yasin's father had been a member of the RDA and the man who had been murdered in the barracoon had been personally responsible for killing him. At the enquiry a white magistrate had accepted Akasaydoo's plea of self-defence. It had been a frame-up, Yasin claimed. Akasaydoo had told the magistrate that he had found subversive literature amongst her father's papers, translations of Nkrumah's speeches and a copy of Lumumba's letter to the Belgian government in July 1960 breaking off diplomatic relations between the Congo and the state that had colonised Lumumba's country and had, under King Leopold I, committed more horrors on the Africans than Amin had in Uganda. Other seditious material that they found in her father's house, Akasaydoo had testified, was aimed at overthrowing the colonial government. Her mother had told her, afterwards, that almost all the evidence had been planted.

Her father had been executed.

At the enquiry, Akasaydoo, who had been about twenty-five, had said that he had killed her father because the older man had produced a gun and shot at him. The GES had put a weapon on display. It had had her father's fingerprints on it. Yasin was sure that it was actually a gun which had belonged to one of the French police Akasaydoo had had with him and that they had clasped her father's fingers around it after he was dead. Yasin and her mother had been in the next room. They had heard two shots. One bullet had been found in her father's head. The second had been found in the wall behind the place in which Akasaydoo swore he had been standing. The three men he had had with him had told the same story. Yasin told Mrs. Quarshie that her father had never owned a gun and would not have known how to use one even if he had had it. The prosecution had then produced another man, an ex-policeman who had been in jail for blackmail, who swore that he had sold the gun to her father. Almost immediately after the case against Akasaydoo had been dismissed the man was transferred from his cell to a position in which he virtually became one of the prison staff. Yasin had sworn to Mrs. Quarshie that her father's death had been cold-blooded murder.

At the end, Mrs. Quarshie reported, the girl had been crying and had said, "P'raps I keel the fat leetle monkey, myself. P'raps in my sleep I do eet because for so long a time I have dream of doing it. It ees why I am here in this house. I give him sex and I plan to take his life. So perhaps that ees what I do, but I don't think so."

*

Quarshie was back sitting on the terrace with a glass of beer in his hand. It was cool and the wind coming off the land carried a smell that was curiously musky and exciting. It was a smell which spoke of fecundity, of a country rich in forests and of land which forced the growth of everything that was planted there, a smell suggesting that what the land had to offer would be an everlasting benison that would always fill the air with the odour of ripening fruits.

Quarshie looked up at the stars above his head and listened to the sea at the foot of the terrace, letting the sight and the sound cool his mind as the beer cooled his palate.

Presently he told Mrs. Quarshie, "There was nothing in the house which could help me. It is all only just beginning. I mean that the facts are starting to slide down the hill towards us but nothing that I can see makes very much sense. Each new case is like learning another language and you cannot make sense of complicated ideas and events until you have an adequate vocabulary. Politics, revenge, rivalry are just words standing by themselves with nothing to support them."

CHAPTER 6

CREDO   To address oneself to the earth by beating on it in ceremonies, by pouring libations upon it, by digging into it and there depositing offerings, by kneeling on it and touching it with the lips, or forehead . . . all these gestures are not directed to the earth but to the power of the ordered universe which it contains.

As for the cross, used by all who draw vevés, whether it is drawn on the ground or traced in the air, its arms are always in balance with each other and one is always a horizontal and the other always a vertical. The vertical stands for the abyss below the earth and the heaven above, thus it stands for the dimensions of infinity. The horizontal stands for all men, all creatures and all earthly space and matter. Where the lines cross is the point where communication between these two worlds is based and the traffic of energies and forces between them is established.

Anton Antibonite looked at the pattern drawn on the flogging block and said, "It's a nonsense, man."

As the Judge had said, the Haitian's appearance was distinctly Rastafarian. He was a heavy man in late middle age and he wore his hair and beard long in dreadlocks. His speech, too, could have been described as modified Rasta and he smelled strongly of cannabis.

His language was Creole, as it is spoken in Haiti, but he could also speak impeccable French.

As he and Quarshie walked from the man's hut towards the barracoon, Quarshie asked him about his languages and in English, with a slight Jamaican accent, Anton had replied, "Born in Haiti, so Creole and French were my cradle languages. Escaped to Jamaica when I became a man. Went to university there and took up with the Rastas. So that gave me English and Rasta. Did an extension course in French at the Sorbonne so that polished my French."

"And your expert knowledge of voodoo?"

"In the blood and the bone, man. It has been the study of my life. I spent five years in your country, where it all started, doing research amongst the people of Adomey. Like in Haiti, every breath of air you breathe in Adomey is loaded with vodu." He pronounced the last word in a way that made "vod" rhyme with "cod," and Quarshie assumed that he did this to make clear the difference between the ancient Adomey religion and the Haitian cult that had developed from it.

Now as he stood beside the flogging block he said, "I know the vevés of my native land and those of yours and I tell you, man, this is rubbish, a game someone is playing."

"Are there any elements in it which could have meaning? Might it be designed to convey any kind of message?"

Anton considered the intricate pattern carefully. "The cross . . . that is common to most vevés. Anywhere that there are messages to be sent to the gods, there you will find a cross. Or if the Invisibles, the souls of all the dead, are in communication with Baron Samedi or with Ghede, the God of the Dead, then the cross is included as a salutation to Him. Some people claim that it is a symbol of Christianity but its meaning and its form are both quite different. In voodoo it stands for a crossroads, the point at which communication begins in all things relating to religion. Crosses and three come up in religions all over the place. In your homeland, three is a magical number and in voodoo the Marassa Trois —*Les Mystères, les Morts et la Larassa*—are a holy Trinity. That belief is as old as our religion itself. So the people of Africa had a sacred Trinity long before the Whites came to tell them that they had one, too. But this is child's stuff." He pointed at the pattern on the block. "Like a child's drawing, you know? Or a child's talk before it learns words. All the sounds are there but they don't make a meaning. The cross can also be a symbol of Baron Samedi himself, the master of the abyss into which even the sun descends, the figure in black who stands at the crossroads at which all men eventually arrive to take the path to the nether-world which accommodates the Invisibles, the dead who still serve the living. Mysteries, man, we live them. The white man thought that when he found science he could solve all the mysteries. But he is singing a different song now, isn't he? Eh?" Anton's teeth shone through the tangle of his beard as he laughed. "Old Whitey is running around like a chicken without a head going nowhere fast."

"Why did you run away from Haiti?"

"The shadows kept chasing me, you know? Little shadows, big

shadows, all treading on my heels, and all thrown by the arch-devil, Papa Doc himself. I tell you, man, that one was poison. Didn't have a gut but a black mamba coiled down inside him where his gut should have been."

"So you ran afoul of Papa Doc?"

"'And one of the elders saith unto me, "Weep not: the Lion of the tribe of Judah, the Root of David, hath prevailed to open the book and to loose the seven seals thereof."' Are you the Lion of Judah, man, that you have the right to make me loose the seven seals? To reveal myself to you?"

Quarshie smiled, ignoring the act Antibonite was putting on for him. "Before you found grounation—that's what Rastas call a conversion, isn't it?" he asked. "Before that, what were you?"

"I was a communist, a card-carrying communist." The man's attitude had changed. He was still relaxed and amiable but now he was watchful.

"There wasn't any future in Haiti as a communist, was there?"

"No future anywhere for a communist, man. No communist could ever come to grounation. Communist is only talking 'bout getting more things. He not talking 'bout his soul."

"All right, what is grounation?"

"It's the affirmation of life through the earth. We black men are closer to the earth than any other people. It speaks to us, man. Sings to us. Don't sing to no one else."

"Specially not communists, eh?"

"Listen, man. I know what you want. For me you got porthole in your head. I can see into it. Man get killed here. Right here on this stone. You want to know what connection I got with him and you believe the connection was communism. Right? Right. I hated his guts. You know? I could've killed him. But I didn't. I'm Rasta, now. I love myself first before I love anyone else. I hate myself before I hate anyone else. If I need to kill, I kill myself before I kill anyone else."

Quarshie said, "And before you became Rasta you went to university in Kingston and in Paris so let's keep the conversation at that level."

Anton Antibonite shrugged. In French he said, "Whatever you want, Doctor. You have the force of the police and the government on your side. I don't argue with the big *bataillons* any more."

"But there was a time when you did?"

"I was a small boy, then."

"What happened?"

"It's in the history books."

"I believe you, but it must be in one of the hundreds I have not read."

"Jacques Alexis."

Quarshie shook his head. "That is not a name that means anything to me."

"Dépestre, Alexis, Faillard, Daumec, Dominique and the two Chenets." Anton reeled off the names as if speaking them aloud was in itself a sacrament. *"La Ruche,"* he added as if that explained everything. Then seeing that he was not getting through to Quarshie he added, "The people I named founded a newspaper called *La Ruche.*" In English he said, "That means the beehive, you know . . . some place where everyone was always busy, trying to sink the boat, not just rock it. Papa Doc's boat. It's a long story. Boat don't sink, don't even ship water. Alexis was one of three sent secretly out of the country to study in France. Afterwards, he went to Moscow. On the way back he came through Sékou Touré's Cotonu, just along the coast from here. Then, when his ship docked in Port-au-Prince, the Tontons Macoutes took him right off the ship. He was thirty-nine. He landed near the Môle Saint Nicolas. It's a public plaza. There he and his companions were stoned. He was a great writer and a great man. He was my brother and I believed in him. They did not kill him in the plaza, only broke his bones and put out one eye. Then they took him away. After, they probably put out his other eye and let him die slowly in some stinking hole in the ground. He was never heard of again. He wrote, 'The trees fall from time to time but the voice of the forest never loses its power. Life begins.'" Anton's voice had dropped to a little above a whisper.

Quarshie asked, "And how does all this relate to Akasaydoo?"

Anton took a deep breath and said, "He and his father were in Cotonu when Alexis was there. They telephoned Papa Doc that Alexis was coming back and gave him the name of his ship. So, like I said, the Tontons Macoutes were waiting for him at the gangway. Akasaydoo was as much his murderer as the Tontons Macoutes."

Now the man was not acting. The unhappiness in his voice reflected true feelings. Quarshie remained silent for a few moments.

Then he asked, "Where were you on the night Akasaydoo was killed?"

Almost contemptuously Anton replied, "First I was smoking the mystic herb with a friend and then I was wit' my woman. Go ask them, don't wait for me to go first and tell them what to say. Go ask them, now."

"And you didn't draw this thing on the stone?"

"Would you ask Louis Pasteur if he invented some cheap patent medicine, or Michelangelo if he painted some crazy piece of pop art? No man, I tell you, it's rubbish."

*

Quarshie eased himself into a chair at the same table where Adedeni Sayonnbo sat alone still studying a massive tome about company law.

When the young man looked up Quarshie asked, "Can I buy you a beer, Mr. Sayonnbo?"

"For the sake of companionship, Dr. Quarshie? Or to lubricate the wheels of your investigation?"

"Since you are a student of law perhaps I should say that it is in the interest of seeing justice done. Would that satisfy you?"

"Frankly, no. I have never found a satisfactory definition of the word, so how can I accept it? But I will accept your offer because I am thirsty and short of money."

"My friend the Judge tells me that you are a talented young man." The Doctor was trying on an approach for size. The response was an amused, slightly contemptuous light in Sayonnbo's eyes so Quarshie shifted his tactics.

"He also told me that you smoke what Mr. Antibonite calls 'the mystic weed.'"

The look in Sayonnbo's eyes did not change much though perhaps it now suggested scorn rather than amusement.

"Is that true?"

Sayonnbo shrugged. "It's on the record," he said.

"Do you ever share that with our Haitian friend?"

"He is a very interesting man, many-sided."

"Were you sharing your ganja with him the night Akasaydoo was executed?"

"So you don't think he was murdered, rather that he was executed. That suggests that he was involved in some sort of capital offence."

"Executed but without having been judged by any legal procedures."

"But nonetheless guilty in your eyes no less than in the eyes of the executioner?"

"It is an opinion I hold in common with a lot of other people about those who use the kind of methods he did."

Again the glint of contempt came back into Sayonnbo's eyes. "Rule number three in the manual of interrogation of those suspected of committing murder . . . appear to sympathise with the suspect's motives. Then, when he has swallowed the red herring, assume you have established a *prima facie* motive and proceed from there. The Judge would not have told you that I smoke pot without telling you that it led to my being involved with the law over it and accused of trading in it. So what do you want me to tell you?"

"Two things. To answer my original question. Were you smoking pot with Antibonite on the night Akasaydoo was killed, and can you give me any proof, since you certainly had a motive and the opportunity to kill the man, that you did not do so?"

"Doctor, the code of law in Bornubia is the British one. Under it I am innocent until I am proved guilty. You have the same legal system in Akhana. But now that you are in an ex-French colony you are, in effect, using their system, which states that I am guilty until I prove myself innocent. Well, I am going to turn to a third code, the American one, and take the fifth amendment."

"Then I must assume that you have a reason for not levelling with me."

"Oh, indeed I have, Doctor, and perhaps it is a good one, or perhaps it is a bad one. Anyway, I want to see that famous sleuth Doctor Samuel Quarshie, M.D., at full stretch without the little help that I can give him. I am sure it will be an impressive sight. Thank you for the beer, Doctor."

CHAPTER 7

HISTORY "Some years ago," a Tobagan planter of Scottish origin wrote, in 1885, "a manager could work a negro slave right into the ground and bury him. Then it was possible to turn around and buy another one. Not any more. Today, against the cost of a sack of sugar the price of a new man is far too high. In these hard times, to make a profit, a slave must last longer before he gets worn out. So either you have to pick only the strongest and best, who are, needless to say, the most expensive, or you have to reduce the hours he works to the kind of time I, myself, spend in the cane fields."

Professor Nigel Sharp said, "So your wife gave you my message, Doctor?" After Adedeni Sayonnbo had left he had joined Quarshie at his table on the patio, saying, "Just the man I wanted to speak to. May I sit with you?" The bright tone of his voice sounded forced.

Quarshie's impression of his companion, as he settled himself on the edge of the vacant chair, was that he was someone whose fine bones, delicate hands and light skin-tone suggested Aryan, East Indian or European blood as well as an inheritance from Africa.

"So you saw someone leaving Darapa's house in the early hours of the morning Akasaydoo was killed?"

"Yes. It was Akasaydoo himself."

"You're sure?"

"His figure is, was, unmistakable."

"And what was the time?"

"About three A.M. I don't know for sure."

"Where did he go?"

"Towards the barracoon."

"Was anyone with him? Or was he followed?"

"There was no one else in the Place de la Liberté that I could see."

"And you think your information is important enough to make sure that I hear it twice?"

"Not really. Though, apart from the killer, I was probably the last person to see Akasaydoo alive. No, I realise that what I saw is unlikely to do more than help you to establish the time of his death. But even that must be some help."

"It is and thank you. Now what else do you want to talk to me about?" Quarshie poured himself a glass of beer.

Sharp regarded Quarshie uncertainly.

"I knew Monsieur Akasaydoo quite well," he said eventually.

"And?" Quarshie was not prepared to be helpful.

"He was not a very . . . friendly man."

"I expect that there would be a lot of people in the Ebony Coast who would agree with you on that point. There are a sur- prising number of them right here on this island. Was he un- friendly towards you—unfriendly enough to make you want to kill him?"

"Of course not."

"But he was not co-operating with you in your demographic studies or whatever it is you are doing."

Again Sharp was silent.

Eventually he said, "I had some private correspondence with him about a personal matter."

Quarshie smiled. "I know," he said, "I've read it." It was the admission he had been waiting for.

"So . . ." The word came out, as sound might come out of a punctured tyre, in a long hiss.

"I know, from your letters, only the simplest of the facts. You are another man on the 'roots' trail but you are digging deep and not just looking for what people want to tell you about your ante- cedents. You are a scientist, you want facts, hard ones, that would stand up in a court of law."

Sharp swallowed. "Right."

"You were looking for the descendents of the people who sold your ancestors into slavery?"

"Yes."

"Did you find them, or did Akasaydoo help you to find them?"

"I was onto something pretty good."

"And he stopped you?"

"He did."

"Do you know why?"

"I think so. The trail was leading to Akasaydoo's own clan. Perhaps not his family but his tribe and even the village his forefathers came from. Akasaydoo could see that this was happening."

"You were, or you are, preparing to write a book about it. And it would not end with those who sold their brothers to the slavers, would it? You would bring your case history right up to date to include the head of the GES who was still prepared to trade in people's lives and liberty. You might even draw some genetic assumptions about criminal behaviour. I'm only speculating."

Sharp said, "You are a clever man."

"No. I suspect I might feel the same way. I might even go so far as to reach the conclusion that when one comes up against the obvious depth of evil that exists in the Akasaydoo family it might be a good idea to see to it that Kofi, the last of the Akasaydoos, is truly the last. Am I still being clever?"

"I only thought of doing it."

"When you saw him leave the house the other night you didn't contact an accomplice, or she didn't contact you—perhaps Yasin, in Darapa's house—you and she didn't follow him to the barracoon and execute judgement on him?"

Sharp settled back in his chair and for the first time looked at ease. "Now you are being too clever, Doctor. Not that some sort of idea like that didn't cross my mind, as I said, but I thought better of it. You see, my book would hurt him more than a knife against his jugular. Others might then be persuaded to do that part of the job for me. There is not much subtlety in cutting a man's throat. That's work for a butcher, not an academic."

"Your people were amongst those who suffered most as slaves?"

Sharp shrugged. "Everyone suffered. I don't think you West Africans can really imagine what it was like. All the books about slavery have been written by men and women from the Americas and the Caribbean, or by Whites—that is, books which speak of things that really happened to us, to our families. They are still happening. No colonial power ever treated you as the slaves were treated in Jamaica in the hundreds of years before emancipation."

Quarshie shook his head and said, "Comparable events happened here. You must have heard how the King of the Belgians treated the people of Congo. There was one French official who wrote, 'The dead, we no longer count them. The villages, horrible charnel houses, disappear in this yawning gulf. A thousand diseases follow in our footsteps . . . We white men must shut our eyes not to see the hideous dead, the dying who curse us, the wounded who implore, the weeping women and the starving children.' Once you've read something like that it sticks in your mind as does the fact that black mercenaries from other tribes were happy to help Whites to do these things. That is why, a while back, I said I could understand your feelings about Akasaydoo."

"So why don't you let the killer get away with it?"

Quarshie half closed his eyes. "First," he replied, "because my own life and that of my wife depend on our finding the murderer. We are completely at Darapa's mercy. So is the Judge and his family. Secondly, using criminal means to enforce the law would be worse than committing the original crime itself because then there would be nothing left but crime and the pestilence which infects criminals and which would soon spread to everyone."

"But the law here is controlled by a criminal already."

"Darapa?"

Sharp nodded.

"Of course, but should we allow that to corrupt us? For me the only way to fight what he stands for is with honesty and the weapons and methods that are at hand. It is the best any of us can do. Do you agree? And if you do would you tell me how you knew that Akasaydoo had his throat cut? That was information which was supposed to be kept secret."

Sharp shrugged. "The staff from the hotel know about it. Weren't two of them used to carry the body out of the barracoon?"

"So they talked. I don't suppose one could expect anything else. And you did not contact anyone after you saw Akasaydoo walk across the Place de la Liberté that morning?"

"I saw no one."

"Have you talked to the Judge about your interest in slavery? You know he is writing a book on the subject?"

"I haven't and I didn't. I know he reads, or works, late at night. I thought he was an insomniac like I am. In fact, just after I saw Akasaydoo cross the Place I went down the corridor past his room on my way to the toilet. As I said, that was about three o'clock in the morning and I noticed, through the fanlight, that he must still have been awake because his lamp was still burning."

*

"Why didn't I tell you that I was still awake at about the time Akasaydoo died?" The Judge put his head on one side and looked quizzically at Quarshie. "For two good reasons. One, you did not ask me. And two, I probably was not awake. I have developed the bad habit of going to sleep with my light on."

The Quarshies and the Judge were eating dinner together. A small group of Japanese were talking animatedly at another table in the large hotel dining room. Around a table near a window some white holiday-makers were tackling their food with less enthusiasm than the Japanese and from the many covert glances they made in his direction, Quarshie assumed that they were discussing him, or the murder.

Eventually, a small, elderly man from the white party got up and came over to stand beside Quarshie. For a moment he glowered down at him and then he said, "I understand that you are Dr. Quarshie and that you are the man who is responsible for keeping us trapped here over this ridiculous murder. Well, sir, I want you to know that time is money and that every hour of every day I am detained here is costing me one hundred dollars and that I shall be billing you, at that hourly rate, for all the time I am kept here. You get it? One hundred dollars an hour." With that he turned on his heel and returned to his own table.

Quarshie appeared to ignore the intrusion, but he did some mental arithmetic. "Two hundred thousand dollars a year is what that Monsieur claims to be earning. That's not at all impossible. And at the going average rate of income in Akhana it would take over twenty thousand men to make that much money in the same time. If and when we get out of this and he sends me the bill I will pass it through the American Ambassador to Darapa. Now, Kwamé, since you were asleep when you should have been awake on the night of the murder and therefore can't help me there, perhaps you have better news about the lists the gendarmes gave you of the people landing on the island the day before Akasaydoo died and those leaving since, if any."

The Judge pulled a sheaf of papers out of his pocket and put it down beside his plate. Consulting it, he told Quarshie, "They really don't offer anything very significant. On the morning before Akasaydoo's body was discovered, the group of Japanese and that charming American with his friends arrived. There was also a group from Arabia, three men and two women. All of them were asked to show their passports and did so. The gendarmes noted the numbers but not the names. Several locals also arrived as did one or two regular traders bringing supplies."

"What about departures?"

"Oh, is that important? Wait." The Judge turned back through the sheaf of papers. "I have gone back a day further by mistake but I see Ponongo left on that day and did not come back until the afternoon boat a full day after you and Akasaydoo had been carted off. The gendarmes, on the morning following Aka's death, cleared the Arabs to leave because they were carrying diplomatic papers and there seemed to be no reason to detain them. A security man was posted to look after them and except when they were in their rooms he had them under surveillance all the time. Most of our Moslems here belong to the Sunni sect and these people were Shiahs. As you know there is a lot of bitterness between them. The gendarmes noted that the women were veiled so they probably came from some highly orthodox sect." He flipped through the papers again. "That's about all, I am afraid."

Quarshie pushed his chair away from the table. "I was not expecting much more. We are attracting too much attention here, Kwamé, let's go to your room and take a look at the facts we have already. Perhaps when we add them up the total may indicate something."

Mrs. Quarshie whispered to her husband, after they had been glowered at by the white guests as they left the room, "I hate this place, Quarshie, I hate it. It does nothing but bring out the evil in everyone."

CHAPTER 8

HISTORY   In Africa drums are virtually as complete a means of communication as the written word. Messages are not sent in some
sort of code, like Morse. The skins of the drums act something
like vocal cords and produce a wide range of tonalities. They
therefore reproduce something which comes close to speech. This
was not a fact that was recognised by the white missionaries. To
them drums only stimulated the African's wicked love of what
the Men of God saw as the libidinous act of dancing.

The white governments were a little more discerning. They un-
derstood that drums could be used to transport messages and that
their contents might be inimicable to the coloniser's interests so
they used the missionaries' objections to have the drumming
suppressed.

Both missionaries and governments were ignorant of, or
chose to ignore, another important fact about the drumming. It
was that the drummers were frequently descended from a long
line of local historians and that when the drumming was
suppressed so was the recording and publication of tribal history.
Thus the Whites' wanton behaviour in this matter has led to the
chagrin of modern Western historians and others who find themselves confronted with, as they see it, a total absence of recorded
history.

Quarshie lay on his back and stared at the ceiling fan.

A faint light coming through the window from the patio outside
was catching the tips of the fan's blades creating a mesmerising
effect that did nothing to stimulate Quarshie's thinking.

Mrs. Quarshie was asleep on the bed beside him breathing
deeply and regularly.

Earlier, as they had talked over the events of the past couple of
days, the Judge had tried to be encouraging but had had to admit
that there was little in Quarshie's findings upon which to base any
conjectures.

For the umpteenth time Quarshie went over the evidence he had so far gathered.

Item: two pieces of a cloakroom ticket. They matched. Why were they in two pieces? As a precaution against the ticket falling into the hands of someone who might use it to reclaim whatever had been deposited? In that case whatever it was could well be important. Stay with that point, he told himself. The sooner you find out what it is the better. But he could not go after it himself. Too many people would be watching him, GES people and De Gobineau's people . . . one group controlled by Darapa, the other by the French. Not to mention whoever it was who had searched Akasaydoo's apartment. He only had Madame de Gobineau's word for it that she did not know who was responsible for searching the man's apartment. Cul-de-sacs, that was the main problem with the case so far, lines of thought which led nowhere.

Nobody, not even the Judge, knew about the cloakroom ticket. But who should investigate that lead?

Mrs. Quarshie said something in her sleep and Quarshie smiled.

"You've talked yourself into it," he told her under his breath. "I'll fix it with the brigadier. Tomorrow you go over on the boat with the market women. Tomorrow evening."

Item: the note on corundum that the dead man had been carrying. Or had he been carrying it? Was it, perhaps, something which had been planted, as so many odds and ends looked as if they had been planted? Corundum, the Judge had told him, is aluminum oxide. In coloured varieties it produces gem stones, rubies, sapphires, amethysts. Otherwise it is commonly used as an abrasive, being the hardest known mineral apart from diamonds. The notes suggested that a discovery of corundum had been made in an isolated part of the Sahel. File that information for the moment, Quarshie told himself, it may connect with something later on.

Item: the doctor's prescription Akasaydoo had been carrying was for neoantimosan, a medication used for infections in cases of bilharzia. This tallied with the post-mortem findings. The autopsy report had also noted that the tissues he had discovered tucked under the mat had stains on them which would have been caused had they been used during sexual intercourse between a male and female.

Item: Quarshie's discussion with Madame de Gobineau had confirmed that Akasaydoo was not in favour with Darapa. Also the evidence that had turned up at the dead man's apartment had,

a) shown that he had extravagant sexual appetites; b) brought to light the correspondence between Akasaydoo and Professor Nigel Sharp.

Item: someone else had been to the apartment looking for something. What? Perhaps whatever it was Akasaydoo had planted in the cloakroom?

Item: the checks on people arriving and departing on the ferry were very casual up until the time the murder had been reported. There had been no check on people arriving by canoe.

Item: Sharp had claimed to have seen the victim leaving Darapa's house for his rendezvous with the murderer. He had also admitted that the thought of killing the GES chief had entered his mind and that he had a rather far-fetched motive for wishing to see the man dead.

Item: the girl, Yasin, had a more understandable motive and she had been less than cool when Mrs. Quarshie interviewed her. Certainly the tissues suggested that a woman had been present at and probably involved in the murder. For his own reasons —Quarshie corrected the thought to "because of his weakness for beautiful women"—and some sixth sense about Yasin, he did not feel that she was likely to have been an accomplice. Mrs. Quarshie had qualified that suggestion when he had put it to her by saying, "She would not, I think, have been capable of playing the role of accomplice in as cold-blooded a murder as this one."

Item: Ponongo. How could anyone find anything sympathetic in anyone with the kind of job he had? However, no matter how unreliable the records kept by the gendarmes of arrivals and departures, in his case they had been specific. He had left the island the day before the murder had been committed and returned on the day after it had been discovered. Did he have any motive for wanting to get rid of his superior? Inside an organisation like the GES, motives, through jealousies and resulting from other conflicts, could well be many.

Item: Adedeni, the Bornubian law student. He had been unforthcoming and antagonistic. Why? Natural bad feelings which often, even during colonial days, had separated Akhanians and Bornubians? Or had he other reasons for not wanting to be scrutinised too closely? Certainly there was a history of bad blood between him and the murdered man. Was his presence on the island really due to the fact that he was being tutored by the Judge? Or was there some other reason for his being there?

Item: the Haitian. He could have drawn the vevé he had described as being "a nonsense" on the stone block in the barracoon. Also, like so many people who had been associated with Akasaydoo, he had solid reasons for hating him. The dead man's actions in betraying Alexis seemed so typical of him, a wanton and brutal love of destroying people on any pretext.

With regard to Antibonite and despite his apparent joviality, Quarshie, in retrospect, got a feeling that the man was concealing a streak of violence.

*

The fan spun on. Quarshie sweated, drowsed and slipped into a bizarre world dominated by the language of drums.

In Africa drums are almost as complete a source of communication as the written word. Certainly drums can spread information much more quickly and widely than messages which are set down in print. This is largely because most African languages rely for meaning on the musical inflection and volume of spoken sounds. For instance, translated into English, an African word may have four totally different meanings yet still be spelt the same way because English has so few tonal subtleties that the change of meaning passes unobserved.

In Quarshie's dream it was the tonalities that were not making sense. The way the drums were telling the story, Akasaydoo was investigating Quarshie, who was pushing a laryngoscope into Yasin's throat. "She must learn to use her larynx the right way," the drums reported Akasaydoo as saying, "or she won't be able to say her prayers properly. It has all got to do with the way she uses her . . ." And there the drums failed because Quarshie knew that what the GES man wanted to say was, "arytenoid cartilage" but the drums lacked the necessary vocabulary. Also there was a bell which kept ringing, overriding the drum beats and Quarshie was saying, "Turn it off, turn it off . . . how can I concentrate with that terrible noise?" when he awoke to find Mrs. Quarshie with her hand on his shoulder saying, "Quarshie, wake up. Somebody wants to speak with you. He says it's urgent." She was holding the telephone receiver towards him.

The voice which answered his gruff "Dr. Quarshie speaking" was muffled as if the man were speaking through a gag.

"Doctor, you must come to the barracoon at once. I have the Judge here and I shall kill him unless you come."

Quarshie wondered if he had slipped into another dream.

"I have already had to kill the men on the two gates. Don't tell your wife where you are going or she might do something foolish which would endanger all your lives. Don't say anything on the phone either. If you don't believe that I have the Judge go to his room. You will find the note there which I sent him to make him walk into this trap. In it I told him to leave it where you could find it. I repeat, don't say anything now, or ask any questions. Don't speak to anyone after I ring off. Just come . . . at once. You have ten minutes to get here. If you take longer than that you will find the Judge dead." The man rang off.

The Judge had stumbled into a trap. Now he was being invited to do the same thing.

As an ex-boxer he recognised the invitation to walk into a "sucker punch."

But what alternative did he have?

He would have to rely on his speed of mind and footwork to get him out of trouble.

"Who was it?"

Quarshie was pulling on a pair of trousers and slipping a shirt over his bare shoulders.

"A man. I don't know who he is."

"What does he want?"

Quarshie was hunting around on the floor for his sandals. With his head down he muttered, "I can't tell you." He yawned. "I have to go out. I'll tell you later. What time is it?"

"About three. Yes, five past three. Why can't you tell me?"

"Because the man told me that if I talked to anyone the . . . the Judge might get hurt."

"Where is the Judge?"

"I can't tell you. Not now. When I come back I'll tell you. Don't come after me, or follow me. That also might be fatal to the old man." With his hand already on the door knob he said, "Don't worry." As he spoke the words he remembered that Akasaydoo had died somewhere around three o'clock in the morning.

He went back and kissed his wife and told her, "Lie down and go to sleep," knowing that the injunction was pointless. "When you wake up I'll be back beside you."

He was out of the door and closing it softly behind him before Mrs. Quarshie had time to reply.

He did not bother to look into the Judge's room for the message that was supposed to have enticed him to the barracoon. Whatever it was it had worked and that was all that mattered.

In the lobby of the hotel the night porter, who had put the call through to Quarshie's room, had gone back to sleep with his head on the switchboard. Outside the gate of the hotel the night watchman was also asleep on a mat spread on the ground so that Quarshie had to step over his recumbent form.

The Place de la Liberté was like a stage set in an empty theatre. A half moon was low over the roof of the police station and a couple of silhouetted palm trees showed their heads above the straight line of the building's coping stones. In daylight the front of the *poste de police* was blue. Now, back lit, it was black and insubstantial.

A long straight alley led to the entrance to the barracoon. It ran along one side of the police station as straight and clearly defined as the parting in Yasin's hair.

Why should she be on his mind at this moment, Quarshie wondered, forgetting his recent dream, and then switched his attention back to more immediate concerns. He must, he thought, be well inside the ten minutes he had been given so he slowed and forced himself to become more alert and observant.

The wall of the barracoon had no windows in it, no apertures at all except the one tunnel leading to the doorway. It was a twenty-foot-high black cliff with the stucco peeling off it.

There was no guard, so perhaps the man had really killed both the gendarmes who should have been on duty. The twenty-foot tunnel led under the cells and a verandah on the second floor and was faintly lit at each end and very dark in the middle.

Should he walk in boldly, or make his entry like a hunter stalking his prey? Boldly had to be the answer. Dealing with criminals and murderers was like dealing with dogs. Any show of fear, or anxiety, excited aggressive reactions.

The moon was too low to cast any light inside the courtyard. Only in the faint penumbra in the centre was it possible to discern even a vestige of form.

If the Judge were in the building he would most probably be in one of the cells or on the flogging block. Quarshie moved slowly towards where he knew the latter would be.

A thin concentrated pencil of light shot out at him from the insubstantial darkness.

Whoever was behind the light made no sound, holding the beam steadily so that it shone directly into Quarshie's eyes.

Quarshie stopped moving.

The beam of the flashlight swung quickly through an arc of about ninety degrees to come to rest so that it illuminated a hand holding a glinting, nickel-plated, snub-nosed revolver. It was pointing at Quarshie.

Then the same muffled voice that Quarshie had heard on the telephone said, "Welcome, Doctor."

The flashlight was turned back on Quarshie's face so that his eyes did not have time to adjust to the darkness.

"I have your friend here. He is lying on the block like Akasaydoo was. Only he is bound down on it as miscreant slaves used to be. When you have listened to what I have to say you can release him. He is uncomfortable but he has not been seriously harmed. Nor will he be, or you either. I am sorry that the same cannot be said of the two gendarmes." The man's English was nearly perfect but Quarshie noted that he said *gendarmes* with a Francophone accent. "They are dead and to save you the trouble of a post-mortem I will tell you how I killed them. With a blow gun and darts tipped with curare. Silent, accurate, fatal. I could kill you and the Judge the same way. But not yet because you have a job to do and my principal wants me to impress on you that it is important. So important that you should know what will happen to you both if you are unsuccessful."

The man paused and Quarshie spoke for the first time. "What do I have to do?" The words came out of a dry throat.

"Find the right man behind Akasaydoo's death. But more important, find out exactly why he was killed and produce evidence to prove your case. My principal believes that there is a document or documents involved. Find it, or them. That is the priority."

The statement had been made out of total darkness. There was nothing Quarshie could see behind the light which remained steadily beamed into his eyes.

Then, like the quick closing of an eyelid, the light was gone and the blindness, which its extinction left behind, lasted so that Quarshie only saw dimly a quickly and silently moving figure turning out of the far end of the tunnel, opposite to the one by which he had entered, that gave onto the beach.

After a moment he groped forward and his hands came in contact with the block. Moving his hands upwards, his fingers came in contact with the warmth and softness of flesh.

"Is that you, Kwamé?" he asked of the darkness.

"Yes."

"Are you all right?"

The old man's voice had a pathetic break in it.

"Yes . . . but my back. He said he was drawing a vevé symbol on it so that you would know he meant business. He used the tip of a knife. My hands and legs are tied. Can you find the rope and untie the knots?"

CHAPTER 9

CREDO First came the sun. It was there when the earth was born and this caused many of the world's earliest human inhabitants to see it as a symbol of divinity.

In the land which gave birth to vodu this primeval power was regarded as a God and given the name of Legba.

Naturally, since it marked man's first moments of consciousness, the sun also marked the beginning of time and therefore the history of the world. To those who believe in vodu the sun also stands ready to mark the end, the final holocaust and it is therefore called Fa, destiny. Thus it follows that, once life began, nature and time must pursue the pattern set by Fa to its inevitable conclusion, death.

The Judge was weak from shock so Quarshie had to carry him piggyback from the barracoon to his room at the hotel. On the way the Doctor again had to step over the night watchman and pass the porter who still had his head down on the switchboard and was now snoring.

Quarshie laid the old man face down on his bed and went and called his wife. He also picked up the few medicaments they carried with them and returned to clean the wounds on the Judge's back. The lacerations were superficial; the knife had cut no deeper than had been necessary to draw blood. Nor was the pattern very intricate by comparison with the one on the flogging block.

"This is recognisably the Legba vevé," Quarshie told his wife as they gently cleaned the Judge's wounds. "Where I come from, Legba is known as the creator, the cosmic phallus. You will see images of him everywhere, especially at crossroads, and he always has three legs, one of which stands as a symbol of his enormous procreative capabilities. In Haiti he also has three legs, only there he is 'Papa,' not young and vigorous but ancient and in need of the third leg as a walking stick. The passage across the Atlantic aged him tremendously. If the man who performed this nasty ritual also saw the third leg as symbolic of a walking stick it could suggest that our Haitian friend was responsible for doing it."

"You couldn't see the man at all?" he asked the Judge.

The Judge had been lying with his eyes shut, suffering the Quarshies' ministrations without complaint.

"No. He came from behind me and in the dark all that I knew was that he kept the barrel of the gun pressed against my spine. He told me he would blow it in two if I did not do as I was told."

"How did he get you to go to the barracoon?" The question came from Mrs. Quarshie.

"My wife and family. They always threaten my wife and family."

"Who are 'they'?"

"I don't know, Quarshie. I only know that if I ignore the threats, they make my wife, or the children, suffer."

"It has happened already?"

"Yes. My daughter disappeared for a week. Kidnapped, kept in a room without a window or any light. First, someone dropped a sack over her head from behind. She was playing in front of the house. From that moment until she was released she never had a chance to see anyone. Food was pushed through a trap in the door. The toilet was a bucket in a box that could be emptied from outside. They came for her, at the end, when she was asleep. We are so vulnerable. All of us. You, too, Prudence. There is danger for everyone. I am old. I would like to end my days in peace but my world, like the world everywhere, is full of violence."

*

When they left the old man's room a little later, dawn was just beginning to pick the eastern horizon out of the gloom and Quarshie said, "I have to go back to the barracoon."

"Why?"

"Because there are two dead gendarmes there."

"Why? I mean why do people have to keep killing?" And then impetuously in the same breath, "I am going to come with you."

Quarshie did not remonstrate.

The dawn was cool and windless and the voice of the sea had dropped to a murmur. In a distant part of the island two cocks were trying to out-crow each other. In other circumstances it might be said that it was the best time of day in Africa.

Neither Quarshie nor his wife felt inclined to subscribe to that view. To both of them the dawn was the herald of another day of anxiety and doubt.

The night watchman was awake now and saluted them, as they walked out in the Place de la Liberté, as if he had been alert and guarding them all night. In one or two other places people were stirring and someone had lit a fire of cow dung which gave the air a sweetish smell that could almost have been incense. In fact, the day seemed to be starting with a benediction . . . except that in a few moments the Quarshies probably would be examining the corpses of two men whose lives had been ended to satisfy someone else's desire to intimidate him. As behaviour it followed an immutable law common to most terrorist activities: to create the highest degree of outrage, attack the innocent and make them suffer. It was a thought which increased Quarshie's concern for his wife's well-being and he said, "I have a very important job for you to do on the mainland. Will you take it on? I can't trust anyone else."

Mrs. Quarshie was instantly suspicious.

"I suppose you think it will be safer there?"

"That, too"—Quarshie knew his wife too well to try and mislead her—"but what is really important is that document the man told me about last night. The sooner we can get hold of it the sooner we shall be free to get away from here."

"And?"

"I have two pieces of a cloakroom ticket. I want you to find out where they originated and to reclaim whatever it is that was deposited there."

He stopped on a corner to look out across the bay towards the rising sun. As it came above the horizon it was as if someone had turned on an electric heater only a few feet away from them.

"We are going to need to disguise you," he added. "Both to get you off the island and again to carry out your investigations." He was dissimulating again. This time with more subtlety and success. Mrs. Quarshie was intrigued and he knew it. Looking at her with faintly amused affection he said, "We'll send you off with the brigadier's wife as a market mammy. Then go to Larronnesseville. You told me once that one of the women who used to come to you in Port Christian had set up shop there. Right?"

"Amelie Bonsu, yes."

"Then go to her. She will enjoy a holiday from her trade and be happy to earn a bit of money looking after you."

"I don't like leaving you here alone."

"Prudence, if there is a clash between heart and head, your heart always wins."

"You're saying I don't behave logically?"

"On the contrary, you are one of the most practical people I know. But love and loyalty win over practicality every time. I can't leave the island. The only real hope of doing what I have to do is to find out what this is all about. Those two scraps of paper may turn up vital evidence. That is the first bit of logic behind my asking you to go to Gambion. The second is that I can look after one person more easily than I can look after two. They have already made you a hostage once and I am sure they will do it again any time it suits them."

Mrs. Quarshie, in turning to face her husband, had to look up into the sun. With her chin tilted up she closed her eyes and said, "I'll go." And waited for him to kiss her. Which he did. "Now let's go and look for those unfortunate men," she said quietly.

*

They were dead. Casualties in a battle in which they had no personal stake. They lay side by side in one of the cells seemingly already abandoned, Quarshie thought, ready for the long, dark night of Baron Samedi. Or should that be of Ghede, he wondered, and looking down at them he said, "It's an academic point which won't interest them. I doubt that they even knew of the Baron, or Ghede."

Mrs. Quarshie looked at him with a puzzled frown and asked, "What are you talking about?"

"It doesn't matter. Look, the poison dart which killed this one is still embedded in his back. They were both hit from behind which suggests that either the killer stalked them very skillfully or that he was someone they knew. We'll go and wake the brigadier and find if these are his own men or whether they are reinforcements."

*

"They are not my men, m'sieu. That is, they are not island men. All men who come under my care are my men. They leave widows and children, both of them. Madame does not speak French?" He was speaking of Mrs. Quarshie. Quarshie shook his head. The brigadier then said a few bitter and ugly words in that language about the murderer. Quarshie nodded and when he stopped speaking said, "I feel as you do about this and about everything that is going on on the island. The sooner I can come to some useful conclusions the better it will be for everyone. To that end I want your help to get my wife away to the mainland. I cannot go myself and there is no one there I trust to do what has to be done. Nor do I want anyone there to know that she is working on my behalf. There is danger there as well as here."

"I understand, m'sieu. What can I do to help?"

"I want her to dress herself as a Gambionaise market woman and to accompany your wife and the other women from the island when they go ashore to market their fish. Perhaps your wife could lend her the right clothing and find a head-load for her? Perhaps, too, you yourself could be on duty when the boat leaves to clear her through the check-point."

"It shall be as you wish, m'sieu. The ferry will be leaving in a couple of hours so we shall have to move quickly. And there will be some difficulty with madame's dress because, m'sieu will understand I mean no disrespect, most of our women are tall. But my wife is clever. We shall manage. You will see." And the brigadier took the Doctor and Mrs. Quarshie to his quarters where Quarshie had to remain to act as interpreter and the brigadier's wife flirted with him to the point where Mrs. Quarshie almost protested.

After a great deal of frenetic activity and laughter Mrs. Quarshie was transformed and enjoying her new costume and make-up, showing her husband what she could do as a flirt. The effect on Quarshie was such that he laughingly propositioned her immediately and she turned him down because, as she told him, her clothing was kept in place with safety pins and because it would ruin her make-up.

The Gambionaise women wear more elaborate styles than any women on the coast. They dress in bright colours and the fashions are quite their own. Necklines are cut low and square and the wide sleeves on their otherwise tight-fitting bodices have many flounces. It is considered chic to wear several skirts, one on top of another, each one a little shorter than the one beneath it, while over all they wear white muslin slips which are clean and crisply ironed. On their heads they wear stiff nylon, or silk, head ties, which are built up to stand a foot or more above each woman's head.

Finally, eyebrows are blackened and continued in a curve down to the cheek-bone, and a blue line is drawn under the lower eye-lids in kohl, or antimony. The palms of their hands, the soles of their feet and their fingernails are stained with henna. The one adornment that had to be left out, in preparing Mrs. Quarshie to look like a Gambionaise, was the tattooing of the lower lip, which is sometimes coloured bright blue.

With all this finery an incongruous note was struck by the head-load she was given, which was a battered old enamel basin filled with red mullet.

*

A little later Quarshie stood some distance from the quay and watched his wife depart. It was an unusually silent departure for both of them, not because they had nothing to say but because neither of them dared to express their anxiety for each other. It was obvious that they were both faced with danger and that it was even possible, given the ruthlessness of the man and his associates who were confronting them, that they might not see each other again.

Quarshie stood alone on the end of the short breakwater which partly enclosed the little harbour. Mrs. Quarshie, though she stood in the middle of a dozen or more women, was as alone as her husband because she could not speak the language of any of those who surrounded her.

As the ferry passed the end of the breakwater neither of them dared to wave in case others watching might be made aware of what was taking place.

Quarshie returned to his room at the hotel with the feelings of a man who is being persecuted for some crime of which he is totally innocent. His feeling of desolation was no less than Mrs. Quarshie's, who, against the throb of the boat's engines, wondered whether she would ever see him, their adopted son or their home again.

*

After he had visited the Judge to see whether the old man needed anything, Quarshie went to his room to sit quietly and reflect on the night's events.

He was not, however, alone for very long. After barely ten minutes he heard someone tapping softly on the door.

When he called *"entrez"* he was surprised to see Yasin slip in sideways and close the door softly behind her.

She was obviously nervous and her first words were, *"Excusez-moi, m'sieu,"* followed by an apology for disturbing him. She told him that she thought she had entered the hotel unseen. She had also been able to leave her own house without Ponongo's knowledge. She knew this because she had looked in through the door of his bedroom and had seen that he was asleep. She had been surprised, she said, to see that he was fully dressed.

She stood in front of Quarshie like a nervous schoolgirl reporting to the principal of her school, with her hands behind her back.

Quarshie suggested that they should have a drink on the terrace, but she insisted that she see him alone and in his room. She was afraid, she explained, of what might happen if anyone saw her talking to him.

Who, specifically, was she afraid of, Quarshie asked.

Anyone, she repeated, anyone.

The first time he had seen her she had been wearing European-style dress. Now she was wearing the native costume of her people from the north, and again Quarshie was excited by her beauty. There was a regal quality in the way she carried herself, the set of her head on her long neck, and now the way the wide dark indigo band on the white cloth she was wearing spiralled up her tall slender figure. All this natural elegance was made, at the moment, to seem slightly false by something he sensed more than saw in her eyes. As she had said, she was afraid of someone, not just of being seen with him.

Quarshie waved his guest to the chair he had vacated and sat himself on the end of the still unmade bed.

Quarshie said, "You've seen something or you have heard something you want to tell me about, right?"

"Yes."

"Heard, or seen?"

"Heard."

"When?"

"On the night Akasaydoo died. I was in my bedroom. Locked in my bedroom."

"You locked yourself in?"

"No. The door was locked from the outside."

"By whom?"

"I don't know. I think Akasaydoo."

"What did you hear?"

It was like trying to make a wooden puppet speak. Quarshie

watched her lips but that only confused matters. Lips like hers should not be paralysed by fear, he thought.

"Did you hear Akasaydoo talking to someone?"

"Ponongo."

"And?"

"A woman's voice."

"You don't know who she was?"

"I can't be sure."

"But you do have an idea?"

"I am almost sure it was Ajua Satay."

"Who is she?"

Quarshie was cautious but, nonetheless, allowed himself to think that maybe there was a faint flicker of light at the end of the tunnel.

"She's a prostitute who . . . who Akasaydoo thought well of."

"Good. You have given me the skeleton of what you wanted to tell me. Now relax and let's go back to the beginning and put some flesh on it. First of all, how did you get into Akasaydoo's house? I mean, you had an invitation, obviously, but how did you get it?"

For the first time Yasin looked Quarshie directly in the eye and told him, "If I came to you and told you I wanted to go to bed with you, would you send me away?"

Quarshie smiled.

"Now, the next question. The records of the gendarmes have shown that Ponongo left the island the day before the murder and came back the day after. So, how could he have been in the house the day Akasaydoo died?"

"I don't know. That's for you to find out. I can only answer questions to which I know the answer. Only you have the reputation for being able to answer the unanswerable." It was said spiritedly.

"Fine," he told her. "Now tell me more about the night you heard the voices. You were in bed?"

"Yes. It was late. I was already asleep."

"But the voices woke you?"

"No, I don't know what woke me up. A door banging, or somebody dropping something. I can't be that sure."

"Then?"

"I heard the lock of my door click and afterwards, very distinctly, the sound of voices."

"And you were able to tell who it was talking?"

"Not then. Later. I went and stood by my door for a long time, perhaps an hour. Then I heard the voices again as they passed by on the landing."

"How long did your door stay locked?"

"I don't know. I went back to bed and I suppose I slept. You see, I didn't think anything unusual had been happening. Akasaydoo used to enjoy himself frequently with women."

"But not with you?"

"I'd rather not talk about that."

"And was what you told my wife really true? Were you looking for a way to kill Akasaydoo yourself?"

"Yes."

"Could you really have done it?"

"I think so. The more I got to know of the man the more I hated him."

"Did Ponongo hate him as well?"

Yasin considered the question before replying, "I don't know. Nothing he ever told me would suggest that he did. They were always in Akasaydoo's office together. When I asked Ponongo one day what they were up to he said, 'planning strikes.' I don't think he was talking about trades unions."

"Do you dislike Ponongo as much as you disliked Akasaydoo?"

"No, because he never did me, personally, any harm. And he could be fun. A good companion, very sophisticated. Knew about lots of things. He had been attached to Ebonese embassies in Washington, Caracas, and Rio de Janeiro. He is supposed to be an expert in South American affairs. He is also a very good dancer."

"When you found that your door was open did you go to Akasaydoo's room?"

"Why should I do that?"

"Curiosity."

"You have an instinct, don't you, for asking awkward questions? What makes you want to know things like that?"

Quarshie shrugged. "I suppose I think of the kinds of things I might do myself. I always want to find out more about people than what they show on the surface. Did you go to his room?"

She nodded.

"Did you find anything?"

She shook her head. "Only a strong smell of perfume. It was something very powerful like *Je reviens*."

Quarshie got up and went and opened one of the jalousie doors which gave out onto a small balcony. The Quarshies were occupying a corner room with one set of windows opening onto the patio and others onto a wide view of the bay and the red cliffs which fronted Gambion's Corniche. It was likely that over there Madame de Gobineau would be checking that the "boy" had laid the table correctly for *déjeuner*. She obviously lived by intrigue all around her and probably enjoyed it. It was likely, too, that she shared Quarshie's own compulsive sense of curiosity about how and why people behave the way they do. It was their business, something which had encouraged their natural appetites for enquiry to the point where it had become obsessive.

He turned back to Yasin.

"Can I trust you, mademoiselle?" he asked.

She shrugged. "I don't altogether myself, m'sieu," was her reply. "The only way you will learn the answer to your question is if you try me."

"True. And I may, one day, just have to do that. One final question. What is the relationship between Ponongo and the Judge?"

Yasin opened her eyes wide. "You don't mean that . . . ?"

"I don't mean anything, mademoiselle. I am just asking for information. Only when I have enough of it shall I be able to decide what is significant."

"The Judge and Ponongo?" Yasin reflected for a while. "I would say it was casual. They don't seem to have much contact with each other."

"Good. I'm glad you came to see me. You have given me a lot to think about."

Yasin stood up and came and stood close to Quarshie looking up into his face.

"It has been my pleasure, m'sieu." Her eyes searched his face a few moments. "You like me, don't you, Doctor?"

"You are a very beautiful young woman. It's in the nature of most men to like beautiful women. Especially men like Akasaydoo."

Yasin pouted. "Why do you have to bring that up?"

"It's just something that I have to bear in mind, mademoiselle, because, you see, I have to tread very carefully."

CHAPTER 10

FABLE And Ananse, the spider, told the bird that had come to eat him, "Bird, do you like the fat white grubs of the chi-chi beetle?" And the bird said, "I find them delicious past all."

Then Ananse replied, "I have a very special supply of them stored deep in this very thorn bush, for I like them, too. So why don't you eat them first. Afterwards you can always eat me if you are still hungry."

"That would seem to be a sensible suggestion," the bird told Ananse and followed him into the depths of the bush with some difficulty, because the thorns were very long and sharp.

"Now, wait here," said Ananse. "The pot in which I store the grubs is in a corner you could not get into. And in case you suspect a trap let me point out that I could not possibly get away because you are much faster on the wing than I am on my eight feet."

So the bird said, "All right. But don't be long."

At that Ananse hurried away and began to spin webs for his very life. Everywhere amongst the gaps in the thorns he wove small tight webs blocking every hole so that where the bird sat waiting, it got darker and darker until he could not see any more and he became anxious and decided to find his way out. But because he could not see he ran into a thorn which blinded him in one eye and then another which blinded him in the other eye and finally thrusting his way out in desperation a thorn ran right through his heart and he died.

So, my brothers and sisters, beware when someone tells you that you are "behaving like a blind bird in a thorn bush." And always be very careful in any dealings you have with Ananse.

The Judge had had his evening meal sent to his room and was eating it when Quarshie visited him. He was sitting stiffly upright in his chair and wearing nothing but a towel around his hips which left his torso bare to reveal a scribble of wiry hair across his chest.

When Quarshie asked him if he was in pain he smiled wryly and replied, "I suppose I can be grateful the bastard did not inscribe his vevé on my buttocks. Also, I am alive. The last man who lay on that block is dead."

Quarshie walked around behind the old man and examined his back. "The cuts are healing well enough," he said, and as he lowered himself into a chair he asked, "Do you think we should have learned anything from last night's exercise?"

The Judge washed down a mouthful of *chu* with some beer before he replied. "Maybe we are dealing with a lunatic but perhaps you had come to that conclusion already?"

"I have been avoiding it."

"Why?"

"It is too easy to write off murderers as megalomaniacs. The majority kill because they're pushed to do it by greed or conceit, or because they are carrying out orders. Before I reach my conclusion I am going to need a lot more evidence."

"I received some documents from the GES on the ferry which docked about an hour ago that will help you."

"Evidence?" Quarshie sounded surprised. "Somebody is volunteering something?"

"It is nothing I asked for, certainly. Why? Does it make any difference?"

Quarshie shrugged. "Whether it does or not will depend on the information. That is, whether they point away from or towards certain suspects. Do they name names and provide certifiable facts?"

"They speak of Sharp and Adedeni. Shall I give you a summary?"

"Yes."

"They suggest that Sharp's activities as an anthropologist provide him with an excellent opportunity to carry out undercover work in Third World countries."

"Who is he said to be working for?"

"Her Britannic Majesty, Queen Elizabeth the second."

"Military intelligence?"

"I don't think so. He seems to turn up in African and other countries when various eastern and western bloc nations are confronting each other and trying to manipulate events. Or he appears where there are development projects financed by other than British funds and sometimes when there have been important new mineral finds."

"Specifically?"

"He was in Algeria doing, it was claimed, anthropological research. There is a picture of him standing by an oil well, dressed as an Arab. About five years ago he was in Pakistan ostensibly to do some research at the excavations at Mahenjo Daro where the Harappa culture was said to be central to his work. But he strayed off amongst the Baluchis two or three times without being able to satisfy the authorities with his reasons for doing so. After that he turned up working for UNESCO in the Malagasy Republic. He was working amongst the Tsimeheti people and he had only been there a couple of months when there were outbreaks of violence against people working for French interests. So once again he was directly ushered out of the country."

"Do the documents cite the kind of evidence that you would accept in court to back up these allegations?"

"Not really. It all seems pretty circumstantial."

"What about his activities here?"

"Ah. I forgot something. First, of course, you know that he was, officially, dealing with Akasaydoo about one of those 'roots' searches but . . ." The Judge hunted through a sheaf of papers he was holding. When he found what he was looking for he said, ". . . Here is what I should have told you first. It deals with one of the masters which puzzled you. The notes Akasaydoo had in his pocket about corundum. He was interested, as were a number of people from other countries, in a find of corundum in an inaccessible part of the Sahel. In the Vallée du Serpent, to be precise. Actually there were really only rumours of the find because the geologists who claimed to have made it never came back and there are suspicions that they may have been ambushed and spirited away or killed. They were a small group of Americans. So far, for some unaccountable reason, the world press has not yet got hold of the story. It's dynamite. Some important information on what happened in the Vallée seems to have got into Akasaydoo's hands. So it then became not only dynamite but dynamite in the hands of a totally ruthless man."

"You said corundum could mean industrial abrasives and gem stones?"

"Right."

"And Akasaydoo had information about the find but the security people, his own people, suggest that they don't know what it was?"

"Yes."

"And he is out of favour with Darapa?"

"Yes, again. And with the French too. From what it says here it also seems that the Bornubians are interested."

Quarshie frowned. "Why the Bornubians?"

The Judge shook his head.

After a moment Quarshie answered his own question. "The geologists who went adrift were Americans, right? So who is America's best friend on the coast? Bornubia. Bornubian oil is shipped to the U.S. So, the State Department would naturally turn to them. Which brings us to Adedeni. What do we know about him?"

The Judge found the papers which referred to the young Bornubian.

"Quite a bit. You are aware of some of the past history. The drug charge, the fact that his father was ambassador here for a long time. Adé spent most of his childhood and youth here. He had a lot of connections amongst not only the younger people but fairly senior people who shared his appetite for cannabis . . . people he could lean on for information. It's all here in the file." The Judge ran his finger down the page. "One other thing is also here. Naturally enough, Akasaydoo did not trust Adé. He had a tail on him from the moment he arrived. So everywhere he visited is on the list. One of them is a known gangland boss. The kind of man you might go to if you wanted someone to carry out a burglary or . . . yes, if you wanted someone, as I believe the Americans say, eliminated."

Quarshie grunted. Those who knew him would have recognised it as one of his ways of laughing. If the information had come in earlier he could probably have told Mrs. Quarshie more precisely what she had to look for. Already that morning Yasin had told him the name of the girl who might have been the murderer's accomplice and thus someone Mrs. Quarshie could track down. He would have to get the brigadier's wife to make another trip to the mainland right away to contact Mrs. Quarshie and give her the new information. Also, of course, he would have to interview Sharp and Adedeni again. This time he had enough information to put some pressure on them.

"What is the name of the gang leader you mentioned in connection with Adé?" he asked.

The Judge consulted his papers. "He calls himself Kwaku Ananse."

"The spider," Quarshie said. "Interesting. That might suggest he is a countryman of mine. *Bon.* Kwamé, I have work to do. Rest as much as you can, old friend."

*

Sharp spun around as if someone had fired a pistol behind his head when Quarshie put his hand on his shoulder. The expression of surprise, or perhaps it was alarm, faded instantly when he saw Quarshie.

"Doctor! You made me jump. I was a long way from the present."

Quarshie had found him on the parapet of an old Portuguese fortress a little way along the beach from the barracoon.

"In the future or in the past?"

"The past, of course, Doctor. My unfortunate ancestors were shipped from this island."

"How do you know that?"

"In my family there is a tale about a child who was flogged by a slaver for not eating. When we were small and fussed about our food my grandmother, and I suppose her parents for several generations, used to say they would send for Captain Marshall."

"Curious. I mean that they should use a specific name."

"I thought so, too. Then I discovered that they had a historical right to use it. I was doing some research into slavery for a paper I was writing. Amongst the documents I read were the minutes of the evidence given before a British House of Commons Select Committee that was considering the slave trade. It was dated the tenth of May, seventeen ninety. Two hundred years ago there really was a Captain Marshall and one of his crew aboard the slaving brig *Melampus,* Isaac Parker, testified that amongst a cargo of slaves picked up here and at Elmina there was a child who would not eat, so the captain had him flogged with the cat of nine tails. A child, mark you, flogged. And that was only the beginning. The child had swollen feet—probably from beriberi and malnutrition. So the captain ordered that the boy's feet be put in hot water. The water was too hot and the skin blistered and came off. And still the child would not eat. The captain said, "Damn you, I will make you eat," and flogged the little fellow again. This monstrous treatment was repeated four or five times over several days. The next part of the statement is burned on my memory so I will quote it verbatim. 'The last time he took up the child and flogged it he let it drop out of his hands. "Damn you," he says again, "I will make you eat, or I will be the death of you." ' In three quarters of an hour the child died. Then Captain Marshall would not allow any of the sailors on the quarterdeck to heave the dead child overboard but called on the mother to do so. She refused and he flogged her. At last he forced her to take up the boy and she carried him in her hands and went to the ship's side and holding her head to one side so that she would not see the child go out of her hands she dropped it. 'She seemed to be very sorry,' Isaac Parker noted, 'and cried for several hours.' And her descendents, my family, remembered the incident and threatened their people with that captain's name. But you know what really stuck in my craw was the thought that none of this would have happened if the greed of certain other Africans had not caused them to sell an ancestor of mine to a white slave trader called Marshall."

"And you believe Akasaydoo's people are descendents of those who made the sale?"

"I do, though the discovery was an accident. Like the discovery that Marshall was the name of a man who really had lived."

"So you were not here specifically to do some personal research into the details of your family background?"

"One does not get university grants for that kind of project, Doctor, as I am sure you know."

Quarshie examined the man who stood in front of him and thought that the Manchu moustache he affected gave him a sinister appearance that was, perhaps, out of keeping with his character, though it might reflect an instinct for the theatrical.

"So what have you been doing? A report I have and your own statements indicate that you have been having a great deal to do with the dead man."

Sharp grimaced. "First, he was a security agent; second, he was a bureaucrat. A bad combination. He saw threats in every shadow though it might only belong to a child."

"And he felt you were threatening him?"

"I didn't say that. I was simply looking for information."

Quarshie fired a shot in the dark. "About what happened in the Vallée du Serpent some months ago?"

Sharp's face remained expressionless. "What happened in the Vallée du Serpent? And where is it?"

"The name means nothing to you?"

"Should it? Are there traces of early settlements there or something? People and their customs and behaviour, Doctor, those are my interests, you know."

"As they were in Algeria, Mahenjo Daro and Malagasy?"

"Exactly. It must all be in the records Akasaydoo kept on me." The man did not look at all surprised that Quarshie knew so much about him.

"But there was nothing there which said what you were up to here except your interest in trying to track down the family who landed your ancestors in the hands of the slavers, and you say that is a project for which you had no funds. So who was paying your expenses? The British government?"

"Obviously I am on your list of suspects, Doctor. Do you think I would have come forward and involved myself in the case by telling you that I might well have been the last man to have seen the unlamented Akasaydoo alive, if I had been involved in his murder?"

"You mean you could not have watched him walk across the square and then have followed him and killed him?"

"For a man with your reputation as a sleuth you are not being very subtle in the way you question a suspect."

"I use whatever method of interrogation gets results. Subtlety is not always the best weapon."

"And have you got results?"

Quarshie smiled. "I have and they are good enough to ensure that you keep your place as a suspect. Thank you, Dr. Sharp." Quarshie turned away then turned back for a parting shot. "Silence, in a case like this, is fool's gold. Perhaps you might consider that fact and decide that it might be wiser to tell me exactly what you were doing here rather than evading the question. If and when you feel like talking I shall always be interested to listen."

*

Adedeni had already drunk several litres of beer with him when Quarshie brought the subject around to that of Akasaydoo's murder. Although the Doctor had been drinking bottle for bottle with his companion there was no doubt which of the two men was the most sober.

"You know," the young Bornubian said, "when you see two strange dogs, I mean, strange to each other, meet in the street, you can tell immediately if there is going to be trouble. I mean, man, you can put out your hand and touch the hatred, it's solid right there in the air all around them. That's how it was with that fat pig and me. Like the feeling there was between the kids and those redneck cops in America's south when they were working on the registration thing. I've read about it and it was livid like the colour of a man that has gotten himself strangled."

Quarshie said amiably, "But that wasn't the reason you came back to Gambion . . . just to express your hatred for the dead man. Or was it?"

Adedeni looked at his questioner through the huge portholes of his gold-rimmed glasses and despite the quantity of alcohol he had consumed there was no misting of the intelligence his glance contained. He smiled and said, "The bloodhound has picked up the trail again. Of course I was expecting it, Doctor. And I promise you it will make life a lot easier for you if you believe me. I didn't do it. That was not the reason for my sharing the hospitality of this hotel with him."

"You had other fish to fry?"

"Right."

"Ones that had to do with events which happened in the Vallée du Serpent or with Kwaku Ananse?"

Adedeni leaned back in his chair, dropped his chin on his chest and looked at Quarshie under the top rims of his spectacles.

Eventually he said, "Of course you're good. I never doubted it. Well, keep right after the killer, Doc, I've got nothing to lose from your finding him. Though I would confess to the belief that the man who fixed him up like that with all those trimmings on the flogging block was doing the world a service."

"Up to a point," Quarshie said, "because the murderer got to Akasaydoo before you had achieved your objectives?"

Adedeni shook his head. "It's no good, Doc. The information you want from me just isn't mine to give. OK? And you won't pry it loose from me, no way . . . with alcohol, with threats, with clever chess-move strategies. So let's drop the subject, right? You've been around a lot. I've got lots of respect for you. You are no mean sculptor: I saw some of your work in an exhibition of Akhanian art in London. And you can sink me any day at drinking beer. So go ahead, see how long that exercise takes. But keep off the subject of Akasaydoo. Then, maybe, if sometime I see a way to help you without compromising my own position in this business, why I will do it with pleasure and maybe even pride. *Skoal*." And Adedeni lowered another glass of beer with a flourish and a skill which approached the standards set by the Doctor himself.

*

Later, when he had written and delivered a note to the brigadier for Mrs. Quarshie, the Doctor surveyed what he had learned so far about Akasaydoo and his death and came to one conclusion: it was like trying to fumble his way through Tutuola's *Life in the Bush of Ghosts* with every approach, or exit, a tangle of spider's webs.

CHAPTER 11

There is a saying in a certain African tribe:

> Wanengena taka
> , La buya badiaboo

> You are beautiful: but learn to work
> For you cannot eat your beauty.

It is an aphorism which mothers tell their daughters and one that few, these days, take to heart. Particularly in the big cities like Lagos, Accra, Gambion, Port Saint Mary, Abidjan, Dakar, Freetown and others, there are many, many women who lead lives in which they are "eating their beauty." It is one of the surest ways to earn the capital to go into even more lucrative businesses.

By evening Mrs. Quarshie had received the Doctor's note giving her the name of the girl who had been in Akasaydoo's house and stressing the probable importance of the documents he hoped she would find. And a little later she had returned to her own national costume and felt easier in mind and body. The many layers of skirts she had been wearing concealed the full natural curves of her hips, thighs and shoulders of which, in a society where such features were much admired, she was justly proud. Also too many of the clothes depended upon safety pins for her to feel secure in them.

Besides, many of the women who sat around her at Le Machin were dressed as she was because they, too, were Akhanians, as was her hostess, Amelie.

Le Machin was one of Gambion's meeting places which catered to the *femmes libres* and their clients. *Femmes libres* are not members of the local women's lib organisation but women who ranked several levels above common prostitutes. They all have education, a flair for wearing fashionable clothes and jewellery and enough money never to have to accept too low a bid for their favours; their intelligence is well above the level of those who hawk female flesh in return for money. Some of the women sitting around the open courtyard under the coloured lights were, in fact, no more than enthusiastic amateurs in "the game" for their own various reasons. There were even one or two white women.

Another aspect of their profession, fairly widespread in Africa, was that they belonged to what might be called a craft guild and treated each other as sisters rather than competitors. Thus they were governed by a code of behaviour which was enforced by an elected hierarchy who enforced rules that made it impossible for any one of them to exploit advantages in, for instance, the type of governmental patronage she could muster and therefore use in the declared price she could charge for her services.

As for the patrons, they were both black and white and usually sat together at all-male tables, drinking. From this vantage point they would examine the merchandise on offer on the other side of the floor and make their choice by inviting one of the women onto the dance floor. During the dance the men and women would weigh each other up. They would then return to their tables and if the man felt that the woman looked as if she could meet his needs he would send a waiter across the room to her with an offer of a drink.

For her part the female had to be satisfied, too. If she was, she accepted the drink. They would then continue to dance together for the rest of the evening and go to his or her house afterwards.

Between dances they continued to return to the group of men or women with whom they had started the evening and the field remained open to allow either party to choose a different companion.

Mrs. Quarshie's association with Amelie had started in Akhana when, in her capacity as district midwife in Port Christian, she had been called in to help after the woman had attempted to abort herself with the aid of herbs and procedures prescribed by an African herbalist. The effects had been near fatal and certainly Mrs. Quarshie had been a major factor in saving Amelie's life.

A feature of the place that might have seemed strange to a Westerner was that many of the women were distinctly matronly in age and shape. It was a fact that was true of Amelie who sat beside Mrs. Quarshie facing three of the "sisterhood." In their own society all were women of standing, leaders of different tribal groups.

The way they were dressed announced this fact loudly. Amelie, for instance, seemed to be covered in gold. Her earrings fitted the auricles of her ears like armour plate so that virtually the whole of the outer rim of her ear was covered. When she smiled she showed a mouthful of gold and her multiple necklaces, bracelets and rings if put together on a scale would weigh over a half a kilo and be worth over $5,000.

For a man of a certain age it would be quite a status symbol to be seen accompanying her, or any of her companions at her table, on the dance floor. By comparison Mrs. Quarshie, dressed in a rich cloth and head tie, both borrowed from her hostess, but without more than modest gold earrings, looked almost dowdy.

Amelie had introduced Mrs. Quarshie to the other women at the table by telling them the story, in all its sanguinary detail, of the service Mrs. Quarshie had rendered her. The kind of experience Amelie had gone through was one of the more alarming occupational hazards of their profession and Mrs. Quarshie's role induced in her listeners something close to an attitude of veneration, so that when Amelie came to the point of saying that Mrs. Quarshie needed help the three women outdid each other in offering to do whatever they could. What did she want of them?

She was just about to respond when a man with greying hair came across to the table. Mrs. Quarshie, assuming that his interest was in one of the other women, sat back in her chair to wait for him to leave and was surprised when he addressed his request to her.

Mrs. Quarshie felt the same consternation she saw on the faces of the other women but could find no ready excuse for not accepting his offer without drawing unwelcome attention to herself.

As she moved around the table to reach the dance floor and stood between one of her companions and the man she heard her say very softly, "Be careful of that rat."

The reason for the warning became immediately apparent when her partner said, "It's a surprise to find you here, Mrs. Quarshie. Especially when I understand you are supposed to be involved with your husband in a murder hunt on the Île de Sintra. May I ask how your efforts there are progressing?"

Mrs. Quarshie was in a dilemma. Her instinct was to deny her identity. But the man was so positive that she knew it would serve no purpose.

As calmly as she could she said, "I don't think I know you, sir."

"That is possible, madame."

They danced a few steps and then Mrs. Quarshie asked, "Then how is it that you know me?"

"Even in our newspapers, here, we have some pictures of your brilliant husband and your charming self, madame. It is the price of fame. May I ask if my finding you in these surroundings means that you have given up nursing, midwifery and the good Doctor to take up the profession to which all the other beautiful ladies here belong? If that is the case I would suggest that they will have to sharpen the competitive edge of their practice of seduction."

He was well-dressed and spoke almost accentless English. Mrs. Quarshie curbed an instinct to slap his face to force him to take the impudent expression off it. Instead she produced what she considered to be a professional simper and said, "If you wish to obtain evidence on that point, sir, perhaps you would make me an offer?"

"You cannot be serious?" That's better, Mrs. Quarshie told herself, and continued to take the offensive.

"You did not answer my question, sir."

"But what a very important and exciting prospect, madame. That is, if I am to take you at your word. Not the least pleasure would be the long talk we could have. Oh yes, indeed, I would make you an offer. Shall we say it would be in four figures?"

Mrs. Quarshie bowed her head with every appearance of modesty and said, "Then I am honoured, sir. However, since I am, if you will forgive the expression, new to this occupation, you must allow me to leave you for a little while to discuss the arrangements we shall have to make with my sisters."

"But of course, madame, of course." And with elaborate courtesy he ushered her back to her table before returning to his own. The contrast in the behaviour of the men around their table and the women around the other, as Mrs. Quarshie and her would-be client sat down, was very marked. At the men's table all the men's heads went up and they looked towards Mrs. Quarshie while at the women's table all the heads came down together like the heads of a group of hens tackling a newly filled dish of corn.

"Who is he?" Mrs. Quarshie wanted to know instantly.

"*Le Crapaud,* he calls himself Quasimodo, the bell-ringer of Notre Dame," said a woman who had been introduced to Mrs.

Quarshie as Claudia. "He writes a gossip column in the *Journal d'Afrique Occidentale*. Your name will be in it tomorrow."

Mrs. Quarshie frowned. The others looked at her anxiously.

"I have to get out of here," she said. "Look, would one of you go over to his table and make a fuss. Say that I am not a member of the circle, that I haven't paid my dues, that all the girls might go on strike, what you like, and stand in front of him, hook him if you can, offer yourself, keep him away from a telephone and stand close in front of him so that he won't be able to see the rest of us leave? Will you do that?" She looked around and they were all saying "yes."

She added softly, "My sisters. I love you. You decide who goes. The others must come with me because . . . because the police are going to be interested in where we are and what we are doing. I am sorry, but that's the way it's going to be. I have things to do. Important things." She was thinking of Quarshie's note. First he needed information on the girl and quickly. Second, if and when she found the papers he had sent her to search for, she was to escape with them to Akhana and deliver them to his uncle, the Permanent Secretary for Internal Affairs. The old man would understand their importance. Quarshie's note had concluded, *"My life may depend on your being successful."* With that one sentence underlined.

No command he could have given Mrs. Quarshie could have had greater force. The great big gentle hulk of a man was the heart and soul of her own life. Without him her existence would become meaningless. So now she was on her mettle as she had seldom if ever been before. In that state of mind she could and would take on all the forces of Darapa, the French and anyone else who was involved in the case Quarshie was trying to solve and, she thought with more than a touch of vanity, she could and would beat them.

CHAPTER 12

HISTORY The man who is brought up in a social background in which he is made to feel inferior and finds himself living in surroundings in which he is accorded rank and stature far beyond anything he merits soon becomes imbued with an almost sublime sense of his own importance.

Thus colonial officials, missionaries, engineers, traders and others who chose to shoulder the "white man's burden" amongst various "primitive" societies overseas soon assumed quite overweening attitudes of patronage. They were attitudes which, in part, derived from the fact that they believed the values they had to offer were inspired by God and stood for progress and enlightenment.

Quarshie leant his huge frame against one side of the inner embrasure of the window. It was a position he chose deliberately because by standing against the light he made his size even more impressive. It also made the expression on his face hard to discern and the expressions on the faces of Monsieur and Madame de Gobineau, the Judge and Ponongo easier to read, because they had to face the light.

He had moved to the window in the first place to counter De Gobineau's move to the chair behind Darapa's immense, if decrepit, desk and take up a position of authority in the group.

Appropriately enough, Quarshie thought, the Frenchman's wife sat beside him on De Gobineau's right. The other two Africans in the room sat somewhat in the shadows on each side of the desk half-facing the De Gobineaus, half-facing Quarshie. Indeed, it was all very symbolic, Quarshie told himself. If his own presence was excluded it defined a house divided against itself in three ways.

De Gobineau was a small, lean man, balding, with a wisp of blondish hair plastered across the top of his rather large skull. He was also unwavering in the attention his pale blue eyes gave to anyone he was speaking to and solicitous and attentive to his wife.

He was dressed in a well-starched white linen suit which shared its unspoilt, clinical immaculacy with the cool, simple white dress his wife was wearing.

Matching this medical image was De Gobineau's incisive way of speaking. It was as if he believed that the knife and an amputation might hurt but was the quickest and cleanest way of curing any infected part of the human body or mind.

"So you thought it best to send your wife away, Doctor. Why?"

Quarshie lowered his head and looked down levelly at his interrogator without replying, forcing the man to bark his question again, "Why?"

Quarshie said quietly, "I think we shall make more progress if we ignore Count de Gobineau's statement—perhaps he is an ancestor of yours, m'sieu—that the absence of intellectual aptitude makes people of my race completely incapable of appreciating the heights to which noble intelligence may rise. So if you will grant that I am an intelligent human you will also concede that you do not get any further with me by shouting at me than by talking with me in a civilised tone of voice. Perhaps a dog will respond to shouted commands. I will not. So shall we start this discussion from there, m'sieu?"

"Doctor Quarshie is right," Madame de Gobineau told her husband quietly. "*Tu sais?* I have formed a high opinion of the Doctor's intelligence from the study I have made of his work." She turned to Quarshie. "Perhaps you felt, Doctor, that having Madame Quarshie here with you made your investigation more difficult? After all, the not-so-very-clever employees of Akasaydoo threatened her and through her, you. Is that not right?"

Again Quarshie waited before replying, this time because he caught a glance Madame de Gobineau threw in Ponongo's direction as she spoke. He, too, could be called one of the "not-so-very-clever employees of Akasaydoo." And the glance suggested that she was looking to see whether the dart had got home.

After his measured pause Quarshie replied, "Of course you are right, madame."

In a quiet, conversational tone of voice, De Gobineau asked, "And you have no other reason for sending her away from the island?"

"I thought, m'sieu, the reason I am being kept here—and I *am* being kept here—is to discover who killed Akasaydoo and why. Is that not so?"

"I am not keeping you here, Doctor."

"I did not say you were. However, your concern over the fact that my wife has left seems to suggest that she should have been kept here, too. Also that her departure is causing you some kind of inconvenience or even, perhaps, that you have something to fear from it, and I ask myself why. Are you afraid that I have sent her to try to discover something that you are trying to conceal?"

This time Madame de Gobineau's glance was at her husband and Quarshie felt that perhaps she could see the discomfiture the man was feeling and was doing his best to conceal. Perhaps, too, she was finding enjoyment in the fact. Again it was she who broke the silence. "My husband is as worried as you are about your wife's safety. Not about anything else. Could we perhaps contact her and invite her to stay with us where, I can assure you, she would be safe."

It was a game and it was his move.

"Thank you, madame. You are very kind, but my wife had made her arrangements without informing me what they are. In Gambion she was going to contact some friends who she once knew in Akhana and then go on from there. There was not much she could do on the island and, as you said, she was a cause of anxiety to me and I have anxieties enough as it is."

"Are your enquiries bearing fruit?" De Gobineau wanted to know.

"You are aware, m'sieu, that it is not in my power to answer that question. It should be asked of *Monsieur le Juge d'Instruction.*"

De Gobineau turned to the Judge with an irritable shrug. "So, m'sieu, will you answer that question?"

"I regret it, m'sieu, but I am under orders from *Monsieur le Président* to report to absolutely nobody but him."

De Gobineau threw his hands in the air and said something under his breath in which the word *foutu* was all Quarshie could hear.

Again his wife came to his rescue. "There is one aspect of this case which interests my husband very much, Doctor. So perhaps you would be kind enough to satisfy his curiosity. It concerns the vevé you found on the flogging block."

"Would you like to see it?"

"We would, and perhaps you could interpret it for us."

Quarshie recognised in Madame de Gobineau a subtle opponent. Every step she took towards one objective was a move in the direction of some other one and he could only stay in the game with her if he made the right guess. He tried one now.

"But of course, madame, but for an interpretation the man we need is Monsieur Anton Antibonite. He is the real expert." And he knew, at once, that he had made the right move.

Madame de Gobineau's reaction was quite correct, quite conventional but he was, he felt, well tuned in to the wave length which related to her feelings. She said, "Of course, Doctor, if that is what you advise. Who is this man?"

"Antibonite? A Haitian . . ." And something of a fraud, was an opinion Quarshie left unspoken. "A man who, as he says, has voodoo in the marrow of his bones. A real expert on the subject."

"Could he have been involved?"

"I suppose he might have been but he has alibis. Pretty good ones. Perhaps Monsieur Ponongo would alert him . . ." Again the game for Madame de Gobineau's benefit. The choice of a word now repeated, ". . . perhaps you would alert him, m'sieu, and ask him to join us in the barracoon."

*

It was a still day and the heat outside made progress as difficult as fighting one's way through one hot damp curtain of muslin after another. Sweat had traced Madame de Gobineau's spine down the back of her dress and had spread like a mound at the base of the trunk of tree where it met the elastic in the top of her bikini briefs, which were visible through the dress's translucent material. It was also causing her dark hair to set her neatly carved features in a tight dark frame that was plastered to her skin. She was, Quarshie thought, an attractive and therefore dangerous woman. Her husband, on the other hand, was the typical *vieux colonial,* a man who seldom saw beyond the surface of things, nor did he want to, therefore he lived with false ideas about his own superiority and the insignificance of all those whom he could force into positions of inferiority. Somewhere Quarshie had read a book describing the abject defeat of the colonials and their military forces by the Japanese in Singapore. It was a debacle which had been invited by, amongst other things, a widely accepted mythology in which the colonials believed that the Japanese pilots could not see well enough because as a race they had narrow eyes and had so often to use glasses. A lot of burnt offerings, in the shape of young Allied airmen, had to be sacrificed before that illusion had been corrected. It was like the beliefs his own people had that they had the ability, given the right protective magic, to be unaffected by bullets though the evidence to the contrary was massive.

What, Quarshie wondered, was Madame de Gobineau looking for in the vevé? Confirmation of the fact that Africans still believed steadfastly in the power of juju? Or was it simply a chance to have a word with Antibonite, a man whose deviousness matched her own. He wondered whether Kipling's *The Female of the Species* had ever been translated into French.

His Canadian room-mate in Montreal had had a poker-work plaque hanging over his bed. It read:

> When the Himalayan peasant meets the he-bear in his pride,
> He shouts to scare the monster, who will often turn aside.
> But the she-bear thus accosted rends the peasant tooth and nail,
> *For the female of the species is more deadly than the male.*

Not all women were bears but he had his suspicions about Madame de Gobineau and watched for any moves that might lead to his being rended tooth and nail.

The brigadier was with them when they visited the barracoon and Quarshie made an opportunity to take him aside to give him instructions about the preservation of the vevé. It also provided the Doctor with the opportunity to tell the policeman to keep an eye on Antibonite and Madame de Gobineau.

At the side of the flogging block she showed a lively interest in the hieroglyphs which covered part of its top surface and Antibonite, like a university lecturer, gave a discourse on the subject. Monsieur de Gobineau looked bored and asked Quarshie to accompany him on a tour of the rest of the barracoon, spending much of his time reading the inscriptions on the walls of the tunnels about slavery.

Contemptuously he said, "For every statement you see here which condemns slavery I could find you one which praises it."

"Indeed, m'sieu?"

"Certainly. A gentleman in New Orleans wrote, 'To say that they are underworked and overfed, and far happier than the la-

bourers in Great Britain would hardly convey a clear notion of
their condition. They put me in mind of a community of grown-up
children, spoiled by too much kindness, than a body of depend-
ents, much less a company of slaves.' "

"And the floggings and other brutalities which no one denies,
m'sieu?"

"Spoiled grown-up children, Doctor. Another man of the age
said in Charleston, 'The slaves do not go about looking unhappy
and are with difficulty . . . persuaded to feel so. Whips and
chains, oaths and brutality are as common in the free as the slave
states. We have come thus far without seeing the first sign of
Negro misery or white tyranny.' I am concerned about such
things, Doctor, and have read much, you understand? So, you see,
all this is a nonsense." He waved at the statements on the wall.

Somebody, Quarshie remembered, had used that last expression
to him quite recently though it had been on a different subject.
Who? He thought hard and it came back to him. Antibonite.

*

After they had completed the tour of the barracoon and Quarshie had seen their visitor on board the police launch Quarshie
turned to the brigadier and said, "So?"

"It was as you suggested, *Docteur*. The Haitian and the Madame put their heads very closely together and she gave him a
packet of some sort. Not very big but something he was very glad
to receive."

"Drugs?"

"I could not say, *Docteur*."

"Find out. Arrest him and the woman for the possession of
hashish. Question them separately and make sure that it is impossible for them to contact the mainland. Also search their living
quarters. I will have *Monsieur le Juge* confirm that order in
writing."

CHAPTER 13

HISTORY Nowhere in the world is the texture of women's society more closely knit than in Africa. God help any male who tries to break through the network of feminine relationships which, for instance, tie together the market women and makes of them a force which has wrecked the ambitions of many a scheming male politician. The same is true of many other institutionalised women's groups especially those formed by the *femmes libres*. Nor is their tight cohesion concerned only with the defence of the group. Every woman in the group keeps up-to-date with the private affairs of every other member of the group. This relates particularly to the love affairs of every other woman in the sisterhood and takes account of their suitor's or paramour's finances, his position in society, the future he is making for himself, his other woman and even his most personal whims and fancies.

The room was full of frills. Cloth frills, paper frills, plastic frills. There was also much carefully ironed white lace and a smell of starch and perfume.

"My workshop," Claudia said gaily as she showed Mrs. Quarshie and the two other women into a cabin on one of the better streets in Larronnesseville. She clapped her hands and a girl of ten or eleven years of age came out of the little courtyard in the back. Giving her money her mistress told her, *"Vas chercher quelques bouteilles de bière."*

Claudia was the latest comer to the ranks of the influential Akhanian women in Larronnesseville. She was also the youngest, brightest and best-educated of the trio who were escorting Mrs. Quarshie and she was the only one amongst them who spoke reasonably good French.

While they waited for the beer she showed them some souvenirs left her by her customers. Amongst the other frippery was an assortment of wigs carefully set out on white, featureless plastic heads. They were hidden from the casual visitor in a curtained alcove.

"They must have cost a fortune," Mrs. Quarshie remarked.

Claudia laughed. "Oh no, Madame Quarshie." She shrugged. "Perhaps ten or fifteen minutes each. My supplier's passions are very easily quenched."

"He is a dealer?"

"No, madame . . . a stealer. I have many useful and interesting friends."

"Good men?"

"Good to me. Because I am good to them. They give value for value."

*

When, after drinking several beers, the other women got up to leave, Mrs. Quarshie said she would stay behind. She told them she had a document in French that she wanted Claudia to translate. It was a pretext which fooled no one, least of all Claudia who, after the other women had departed, said directly, "You wish for information about Ajua Satay?"

Because Mrs. Quarshie looked surprised the younger woman added, "Smells come to us on the air we breathe, why should not information? All sound is only vibration. The wind carries the thunder of drums many miles. Everyone here knows that Ajua was a friend of Akasaydoo. He had picture books from America which show how men and women behave together there. He used to invite Ajua to prove to him that what white men and women could do black men and women could do as well. Her association with that man made her very rich. She is a woman without scruples."

"You knew her well?"

Claudia shrugged. "What is well? Like fish that swim together in a shoal know each other? Or goats that belong to the same herd?"

"When did you last see her?"

"More or less two weeks ago."

"Do you know where she lives?"

Claudia again called the girl who worked for her. As the child came in she made a little curtsey to Mrs. Quarshie, then turned to her mistress, who asked her for Ajua Satay's address. "The girls who work for us play together a lot and know everything that is going on," Claudia told Mrs. Quarshie as the child ran off to get the information her mistress requested.

On her return the girl spoke rapidly to Claudia who translated for Mrs. Quarshie. "Ajua used to live on the Rue de Paris but she has left. She went in a hurry and it is said that she returned to Akhana."

Mrs. Quarshie frowned. "Of course I could have her traced there but that would take time we don't have. She must have left an address with somebody."

Claudia said, "The bank. All our people here keep their money in the Bank of Akhana. Perhaps someone there knows her home address."

Mrs. Quarshie looked at her companion speculatively. After a moment she said, "Would any of your wigs fit me? You see, people will be looking for me."

"Of course, of course. They are yours. Try them all." Claudia bubbled over with enthusiasm and, rattling the mass of coloured bracelets she wore on her arms, she helped Mrs. Quarshie try on a half a dozen wigs.

The fitting ended with Mrs. Quarshie following both her natural instinct and her sense of caution when she chose the least flamboyant.

"I don't want people to notice me," she said. "If I could disguise myself as a mouse I would."

To Claudia the idea of Mrs. Quarshie as a mouse was hilarious though she agreed that her guest's strategy was correct.

The women, both very modestly dressed, arrived at the bank where Claudia had an account and they were taken in to see the Akhanian manager.

When Mrs. Quarshie revealed her identity the manager got up and quietly closed and locked the door of his office.

As he sat down again he said, "The police have already been in contact with me to enquire if you had been in to draw money. I take it you and your husband are involved with . . . with the events on the Île de Sintra. No secret police force likes to have their *patron* liquidated."

"But we did not do it," Mrs. Quarshie expostulated. "We are trying to find out who did."

"Madame, this is the Ebony Coast. Did you ever see a nest full of vipers? There is no way of telling which one will bite you and why; particularly why. For instance, you step on a tail but you don't know which head it belongs to. All you know is that you have been bitten and are dying. So be very careful. Now what can I do for you? I hope it is nothing too risky, or difficult."

Mrs. Quarshie said, "I understand your anxiety, Mr. Ijason"—the man's name was on a tablet on his desk—"and I am sure Colonel Jedawi will appreciate your willingness to help us." It was widely known that Quarshie reported directly to Akhana's President.

"Ah. So our country is also involved in this business? I had not realised that."

"To the extent that one of our nationals could well be an important witness."

"So? Do I know her?"

"Ajua Satay?"

For a moment Mr. Ijason looked apprehensive. Then he said, "Our relationship was a business one." It was a statement which could have been taken either of two ways. Mrs. Quarshie chose to ignore the one which might have had the more personal implications.

"Good. However, you may not know that she has left the country."

"So? And you will want me to check if her account is still open or whether it has been transferred. It would be better if I dealt with that matter myself." He came out from behind his desk.

"Thank you. What is most important, sir, is whether or not she has left a forwarding address and if she has what it is. Would it be difficult to answer that question?"

"Not difficult but unethical." Mr. Ijason smiled slightly. "I would deny having given it to you in a court of law. But we do not, I think, need to cross that bridge until we come to it."

After he had left the room Mrs. Quarshie moved uneasily in her chair and asked her companion softly, "Do you trust him?"

Claudia replied grimly, "From the sisters in our community I could find out enough about the man's dealings to have him deported if not thrown straight into jail. And he knows it. My profession has other benefits besides a way to get free wigs. He won't make any false move."

*

Back in her new friend's cabin, with Ajua Satay's address in Akhana, Mrs. Quarshie said, "I hope the next task I have to do will be as easily accomplished as that one." She produced the two pieces of the cloakroom ticket and explained what was required.

Claudia looked at the little pieces of green paper. "There are a lot of clubs and cinemas with cloakroom tickets like that," she said.

Mrs. Quarshie turned the ticket over. "It says on the back, 'Pam Pam.' That's a cinema, isn't it?"

"I could find out."

Mrs. Quarshie looked at the younger woman in silence for several moments then slowly shook her head.

Claudia opened her eyes wide. "You don't trust me, do you? You don't trust me?" She sounded shocked.

"You must forgive me." There was a hint of anguish in Mrs. Quarshie's voice. "I dare not. My man's life depends on . . . on my not making any mistakes. Can you understand that?"

Claudia shrugged and answered, "I wish I could. Men are useful. I work for them and they pay me. I belong to myself and to no one else. You see? It is much simpler that way. So you want to go and try the Pam Pam yourself?"

Mrs. Quarshie shook her head. "They would wonder why I came to collect something which they know belonged to someone else. No. I said I wished it was going to be simple. It's not simple. Oh dear."

After a moment Claudia said, "If you have the right connections it is."

Mrs. Quarshie brightened.

"But you are going to have to trust me at least a little bit."

Mrs. Quarshie waited for Claudia to continue.

"One of my clients is a corporal in the police."

Mrs. Quarshie shook her head.

Claudia shrugged again and said, "Well, you think of something better."

Miserably Mrs. Quarshie told her, "I can't. But we have to make sure he can't trick us. That he can't get away with whatever it is he is given in return for the ticket."

Claudia moved from place to place around her room picking up and putting down first a paper hibiscus and then an ebony crucifix and after that a cunningly reassembled skeleton of a frog. She took it from its place on a dresser beside a tuft of red feathers from the tail of a grey African parrot.

"Medicine, ma," she said suddenly, picking up the feathers and turning to Mrs. Quarshie. "Big medicine." She was talking of magic. The red tail feathers from an African parrot are highly regarded for their powers in relation to wizardry.

"This one,"—she indicated the feathers,—"tells me how we do it. We make it a game."

Mrs. Quarshie was doubtful whether making a game out of anything as important to her as her mission was a good idea.

"My corporal is still a good man to pick up whatever it is Akasaydoo left at the Pam Pam, no? But you are afraid he might run away with it. In my game if he did that he would have to run away with me, too. You still look doubtful. Of course, because that's where the game comes in. We pretend he had arrested me and . . . *and* I am chained to him by handcuffs." Claudia looked triumphant. "It would be difficult for either of us to run away then, wouldn't it?"

Mrs. Quarshie was still cautious. "Why would he arrest you?"

Claudia snorted, "Oh, for any one of a thousand reasons. A client could have claimed that I had cheated him, or I might be charged with receiving stolen goods, or I might have failed to pay my taxes, or the GES might suspect that I have been passing information to espionage agents or . . . Is it enough?"

Mrs. Quarshie nodded. "And you think the corporal will play this . . . this game?"

"Mama, if I cannot make him do something like that for me I will find a job with the little girls serving the other sisters to learn my business again."

"Then we must get this young man here at once. He is young?"

Claudia shook her head. "That is one of the holds I have on him, mama. He is old. Ones like him find it hard to afford women like me. He has three wives."

Mrs. Quarshie stood up. "Then you will want me out of the way. Do you think you will be able to get him to come now?"

"I will send the girl to the police station. He will come straight off duty just after dark."

"You can be that sure of him?"

Claudia laughed. "Can you imagine how his wives would behave if I went to them and told them how often he comes to see me? We women, here, have been too long the toys and slaves of men. They have used us. Now I use them. Besides, in this profession we often have information the police need. My old friend the corporal does not have much in his head, much intelligence. But they keep him on because every now and then he brings in interesting reports. Material I give him. It is a process which works two ways because quite often he brings me information the sisters need to know."

*

The corporal had a grizzled beard which he had not shaved for a couple of days and his attitude towards Claudia, Mrs. Quarshie thought, was more that of a father with a daughter than a man with a lover.

What happened between them Mrs. Quarshie could only guess. Whatever it was it worked as Claudia said it would.

Mrs. Quarshie was told to wait in the courtyard with Claudia's maid until she heard the front door of the cabin slam. Then she was to follow them at a discreet distance.

To pass the time Mrs. Quarshie talked to the girl and found that her name was Lucille. Communication between them was slow because they had no common language. However, a few shared words of French were sufficient for Mrs. Quarshie to discover that the child thought her employer was good to her. She showed Mrs. Quarshie her tiny room, which was furnished with a sleeping mat, a wooden box which served, when it might be required, as a seat or a table and, luxury of luxuries, a small pillow. Beyond that, all that the room contained was a candle standing in the lid of a tin. "Food?" Mrs. Quarshie asked, *"Man-ger?"* And she gestured towards her mouth with her fingers closed. Lucille nodded, *"Bien oui!"* And then the front door of the cabin slammed and Mrs. Quarshie hurried across the little yard into the back door and, quietly, out of the front door into the street.

She was wearing a cover cloth with a dark blue and black pattern on it which blended into the darkness of the streets in the *bidonville*. The corporal was in uniform and was already handcuffed to Claudia.

For the most part the streets they took had no lighting and Mrs. Quarshie had to keep quite close so as not to lose sight of them both.

After about a mile and a half they came out into the centre of the town which, by contrast with the area they had just left, blazed with light.

The corporal and Claudia walked very close to each other holding hands and the steel band around the prostitute's wrist mixed with the bangles she was wearing to become one of them. They walked on the outside of the sidewalk well away from the brilliantly lit windows and the displays of imported goods. Over the windows tubes of fluorescent light added garish colours to a scene which might have been typical of any major shopping thoroughfare in any capital city in Europe, or America. The air was full of the stench of Gauloise and Gitanes cigarettes mixed with exhaust fumes from the dense pack of cars, which competed with each other for the available space on the paved highway.

Amongst the pedestrians the few white faces sifted through the Blacks like pink marbles sifting through those of many much darker shades.

In these surroundings Mrs. Quarshie could drop back a little keeping the distinctive uniform cap of the corporal in view quite easily.

The canopy, with its many electric light bulbs announcing the name Pam Pam in red against yellow, eventually appeared, and the corporal and Claudia turned across the sidewalk and went inside.

Mrs. Quarshie was suddenly seized with anxiety. Might there be another door through which they could leave the building and evade her? Somewhere in the recesses of her mind a doubt lingered. Why? she asked herself. Surely Claudia was trustworthy. What could she herself do if, with her police escort, Claudia did not reappear soon? She edged forward and moved into the entrance standing just inside the arch pretending to read the advertisements though they were in French and meaningless to her. The cloakroom would, of course, be in the foyer, or somewhere inside. A white couple, talking animatedly about the film, pushed open a swing door close beside Mrs. Quarshie, who felt an icy gust of air-conditioned air envelop her. She tried to catch a glimpse of the foyer again before the door closed but only saw a large semicircular counter loaded with candies, peanuts and popcorn.

Then another thought, as terrible as the previous one, struck her. What if they could make a copy of whatever it was they had to pick up, perhaps some papers, or a message of some sort?

After a further moment's hesitation she made up her mind. She would have to go in and see. She pushed open the door and was forced to catch her breath as the blast of cold air struck her again.

Except for the girl behind the candy counter she saw no one. Facing her were two entrances leading out of the lobby into the auditorium. Over to the right there was a door labeled *"Ves-tiaire."*

She was just starting to move towards it when it opened and rather awkwardly, because they were still chained together, the corporal and Claudia came out. Mrs. Quarshie turned quickly and pointed towards a bar of chocolate on the candy counter. She almost snatched her purchase and did not wait for her change. She could not risk losing sight of Claudia and her companion. Outside she believed for a moment, because she could not see them, that they had chosen to walk in the opposite direction to the way they had come. Then she saw the uniform cap and hurried after it. When she had caught up sufficiently to observe them closely she was disturbed to see that the corporal was carrying a heavy rain-coat. She had been expecting a briefcase, or a thick envelope.

When they reached Claudia's cabin the policeman handed the raincoat to his companion, unlocked the handcuffs and departed.

As soon as he was out of sight Mrs. Quarshie knocked and Claudia admitted her.

Wordlessly she proffered her guest the raincoat. Then, as Mrs. Quarshie took it, she said, "The attendant told us a small fat man with glasses had left it." He had, she told them, given her a big tip and had suggested that someone else might be coming to collect it. "That was three weeks ago."

Mrs. Quarshie quickly looked through the pockets and then repeated the exercise but found nothing.

She removed her wig, as if to give her intelligence more room to manoeuvre, and sat down.

Claudia said, "A false trail?"

"No," Mrs. Quarshie answered her, "no. It can't be. Quarshie was so positive. It means so much to him. And to me. There must be a message somewhere."

Claudia put on the raincoat. "My, it's heavy," she said. "Imagine having to wear something like this."

She was twisting this way and that in front of a long mirror. Then she turned and looked at her back view over her shoulder.

Mrs. Quarshie stared at the front of the coat sullenly. Suddenly she was on her feet saying, "Stand still. Stand still."

"What?"

"The buttons."

"What about them?"

"They were never sewn on by a professional. Look. They are

not even in line." She spun Claudia so that she could see herself in the mirror. "And the stitching. They are not properly sewn on at all. Has the coat a lining?" It had. "And look how badly it has been sewn up. That was never sewn by anyone who knew what they were doing. Scissors. Get some scissors."

Their first discoveries were totally unexpected. Behind each of the top buttons they found two French thousand-franc notes held in place by stitching. The coat was belted and had shoulder straps and a double row of buttons on the front. There were cuff straps with buttons as well. In total the value of the money they found tacked inside it came to the equivalent of close to $5,000. More important, however, was a small slip of paper. On one side there was a woman's name, Ama Kusunu, and what appeared to be the name of a village, Bondooko. On the other side were several hieroglyphics which Claudia recognised as being the symbols that had been used throughout the country during the last elections. For those who were illiterate and had to vote, the symbols—a palm tree, a round thatched hut, a hoe, the horned head of a local cow and finally a cutlass, or machete—were used to represent each of the political parties standing in the elections. Darapa's party, very appropriately represented by the machete, had won the election by an overwhelming majority.

Both women were perplexed as to the use the symbols might have until Mrs. Quarshie tapped the piece of paper with her index finger.

"Identification," she said, "that's it. Mama Ama Kusunu is probably illiterate. If she has something to hand over she must know that the man or woman who has come to ask for it is the right person. I have to go to see her. Are you going to come with me? Where is Bondooko?"

"Yes. I don't know." Mrs. Quarshie's excitement was infectious. "We'll have to find out at the lorry park. You're sure you don't want to sleep a little first?"

Mrs. Quarshie yawned and said, "It would be nice. But I wouldn't shut an eye. How could I? With Quarshie in danger and depending on me."

Though she did not know it, events which were happening at just about the same time on the Île de Sintra were proving that, for the moment at least, Quarshie could well take care of himself.

*

Twenty minutes later, when the two women left the cabin, neither of them saw a man slip out of the shadows further down the road and, keeping a discreet distance behind them, follow them towards the lorry park. Nor did they notice him close by in the press of people around them when, as the first streaks of dawn appeared in the sky, they asked which lorry they should take to get to Bondooko.

CHAPTER 14

HISTORY A man who made a close study of the Bantu people, Father Placeid Tempels, found that they had an exceptionally strong sense of morality. To support their concepts in this matter they had made a very serious study of human wickedness. One of their findings pointed to the fact that a man, against his better instincts, could be provoked to the point where he could ignore this instinct and become a murderer.

"How did it happen, Doctor?"

The brigadier glanced up at Quarshie, having examined the dead man at his feet. The policeman had again been pulled from his sleep to examine a corpse.

"I killed him," Quarshie said unemotionally, "after he had tried to kill me with that cutlass." He looked out to sea where the reflection of the last stars were still glittering faintly on the water.

"Yes, m'sieu, continue," the brigadier prompted gently.

"I had much on my mind and woke very early. The hour before dawn is the finest time to think, or to meditate. A sandy shore and a quiet sea added to the silence help to create the right mood. So I was walking along here barefooted . . . see, I am still without shoes? The moon was bright and low. I had my back to it and the sand was very white. As many men do as they walk and think I was looking down at the ground. Presently I was aware that someone was close behind me, a little to my right, because I saw his shadow to my left but, you could say, overlapping mine. Then I saw him raise something—it could have been a club—over his head to strike me. I was once a boxer, my friend, and I have not lost much of the speed of my reflexes. As he struck, two-handed, I side-stepped and he buried the cutlass deep in the wet sand as you see it now. He was bent forward and off balance as I turned and struck him. The blow was delivered like this with the hands clenched together as if in prayer. I struck downwards with all my strength at the back of his neck. I am strong, and he died because

I broke his neck. It's a simple story, is it not? And the facts are written here in the wet sand. His footprints and my footprints. I went to that hut afterwards and woke the woman in it and sent her for you. That, too, is written in the sand. See? Do you know the man?"

"Yes, m'sieu. He is one of my men. Or rather one of those who were sent me as a reinforcement from the mainland. I believe he is, or was, a member of the GES."

Quarshie nodded. "That would be probable. I wonder if he was taking orders from somebody on the island, or whether he was sent across from Gambion to kill me?"

"That is a question, m'sieu, he will never answer." The brigadier bent and turned the dead man on his back and his head rolled loosely to one side. Then the policeman went and looked at the cutlass where it stood in the sand. After a moment he said, "I am glad, m'sieu, you made him miss. If he had struck home he would have divided your head into two pieces, such was the force of the blow which buried the cutlass this deep."

CHAPTER 15

HISTORY Individually and in groups African women have often shown that though they may give the impression of being meek and subservient, when they do unleash their instincts they are fully prepared to treat men to the same violence that men may practice on them. Don't ever forget that one of the most feared armies the world has ever seen was established by the King of Dahomey and that all its members were women.

Most of the passengers on the mammy-wagon were, as the name suggests, women. They were almost all traders at that time in the morning, transporting their wares out to villages where there were few if any stores, and the main bulk of the merchandise people needed was bought and sold in the market-places. They were carrying plastic utensils of various kinds, cloth, imported canned foods and other manufactured items. Those going to nearby villages would return in the evening with fruit, vegetables, palm oil and other country-grown foodstuffs.

There is no pandering to comfort in a mammy-wagon. The seats are thick, narrow planks set in slots across the back of the truck with only enough space between them to fit the passengers' legs, so long as they keep them bent downwards from the knees at right angles. Most women prefer to take whatever they are carrying inside the truck, although those with conglomerations of plastic buckets and other items in nets or other bulky packages are more or less forcibly separated from their goods by the driver's assistant. The packages are then secured on the roof of the vehicle in a rack where the load gradually assumes unlikely proportions.

On the rare occasions when Mrs. Quarshie travelled in a mammy-wagon she paid first-class fare and rode in the front beside the driver. There she would have a padded seat and the protection of the windshield and side windows, when these could be closed without everyone inside dying of the heat.

On this trip she wanted to be as inconspicuous as possible.

with Claudia, she joined the rest of the travellers in the back. There, there was a roof but the sides were wide open to the dust-laden wind and frequent rain storms. Some mammy-wagons had canvas screens which could be lowered, but generally the heat generated by the tightly packed passengers soon became unbearable and the passengers preferred to get wet, even soaked, so that when they got off the truck at their destination they looked as if they had walked out of a river.

About twenty miles out of Gambion, at their first stop, everyone got off the lorry to ease their already cramped legs and suffering buttocks.

The vehicle always parked in the village's market area and Mrs. Quarshie was the first to notice that wherever they circulated amongst the stalls the same man was never far distant.

She pointed this out to Claudia, who turned and looked back boldly in the man's direction. One quick look was enough. She turned to Mrs. Quarshie and told her, "I know that man. The corporal is a fool. I told you, didn't I? He has put one of his own men on to follow us."

"You're sure?"

"Certain. That is, *if* he is following us. We will be able to prove that at the next stop."

Mrs. Quarshie, now that she was faced with some tangible threat, reacted characteristically. She said, "Then we shall have to deal with him." It was a clear and simple affirmation of fact.

Claudia looked at her in surprise.

"We have several stops to go, don't we?" Mrs. Quarshie con-

ave time to consider how to do it."

*

v wandering away from the market-place some huts, they were able to prove the them.

orporal has told him to protect

y way concerned with our busi-
oluntly. "When did you last see the

"He came to my door with the corporal last night and then went away without saying anything."

"And you weren't suspicious?"

"No. I thought of him as one of the corporal's friends."

"And if someone else is using the corporal? From what you say he could be quite stupid enough to bring the man with him to show him where you lived. Could one of the other sisters have told the police I was here staying with you the same way you give the police useful tips? Or perhaps the bank manager is so afraid of his nest of vipers that he placates them by throwing them titbits, like you say you do." She wanted to stamp her foot and say I knew I was right to feel uneasy.

Instead she said, "All right. Now we know the worst, we can be ready for it. We must go back to the lorry and at the next stop we will make our preparations."

*

They had travelled close to seventy miles and were in a thickly forested area when Mrs. Quarshie gave the operative order. "At the next stop just as the lorry starts to move, jump off."

It was a small village which suited Mrs. Quarshie's plan admirably. By not getting off at the market-place the two women were able to hold outside seats on opposite sides of the bus. At a previous village they had each bought one of the short replacement handles that are used for hoes. These are about two inches thick and two feet long, and they were carrying them concealed in the outer wrapper of their *panjas*. Just as the bus started to move they both dropped off, throwing their shoes ahead of them. They waved the driver on and since he had been paid he accepted the order without demur, writing it off as another example of female unpredictability.

Not so the policeman. He too had to leap off but it took him several moments to climb over various people before he could reach the side of the truck.

By the time he was on the road he was just in time to see Mrs. Quarshie and Claudia moving off rapidly in opposite directions.

It was a moment of agonised uncertainty for him before he decided to follow Mrs. Quarshie.

The plan Mrs. Quarshie had worked out allowed for two contingencies. The man might carry on with the bus. In that case he would have had to wait in the market-place at Bondooko for them to arrive and they, following him, would arrange for their transport, whatever it was, bus or taxi, to drop them on the outskirts of the village and thus enter it without his seeing them.

Or, as it happened, he would get off when they did and be confused by their separating and have to decide to pursue one of them.

Most villages along a highway, such as the one the bus had just started to leave, act as communication centres for other villages out in the forest that are inaccessible to motor traffic. This village was no exception, a factor upon which Mrs. Quarshie had been relying. The links with the outlying villages are simple footpaths through the dense forest.

The area was at the centre of a basin of hills and a storm was brewing. Thunder and lightning wandered about in the sky muttering threats.

Mrs. Quarshie was no longer in a hurry. The bait had been taken so it was up to her to play the catch.

Most of the villagers, anticipating the potential deluge, were already inside their huts and there were few, if any, spectators of the small procession of first Mrs. Quarshie, then the policeman, finally, cautiously following the other two, Claudia.

For ten or fifteen minutes the three of them, one behind the other, Claudia always keeping a bend in the track between herself and the policeman, continued to move away from the village.

Then the storm broke and the rain came down in a vertical wall of water that was several miles in thickness. The natural thing to do would have been for the three people trailing each other along the path to have moved away from it into the shelter of the thick roof of trees.

But the situation was one in which a natural sequence in the events would be unlikely, since they were being controlled by the kind of determination Mrs. Quarshie could bring to bear on a situation.

After she had rounded a bend in the path which concealed her from the policeman, she turned with her short hoe stave in her hand, and met him as he came round the corner.

Half blinded by the rain he did not appreciate what happened until he was almost on top of her.

It was a confrontation which verged on the comic because neither of them had more than a word or two of any language in common.

With her baton at the ready to strike him, Mrs. Quarshie shouted, *"Non."*

The policeman said, "Yes," and then again, "yes."

Mrs. Quarshie waved her heavy stick and repeated, *"Non."*

The policeman broke into a torrent of words that were barely audible above the sound the rain drew from the leaves of the trees, a sound like that of a swift river pouring through rocky rapids.

All of which meant that when Claudia's attack from behind came it was a total surprise. She stepped up to her quarry stealthily and with a sweeping blow, as if she were using a sickle to cut grass, she used the stick to strike his right ankle.

He screamed, half turned to his right and Mrs. Quarshie chose that moment to strike his left elbow with all her strength.

The man screamed again and from trying to clutch his injured ankle he snatched at his left elbow. Meanwhile the rain thrashed down on his bent back while his screams turned into a pathetic mewling cry like the sound made by a sick baby.

Mrs. Quarshie's attitude changed instantly and she put her arm around his shoulder and said in her own language, "You poor man. You poor, stupid man."

To Claudia she said, "You did well, my daughter. Now we will take him and leave him nearer the village so that when this rain is over he will be able to get help."

*

Later, they found a woman in the village who sold cloth and they traded their soaking wraps for some cheap locally produced material. Then, when the storm was over they crowded into an already overloaded Peugeot 404, which they managed to stop as it passed through the village, and were soon in Bondooka.

There they made enquiries for Ama Kusunu and were directed to a house built of concrete blocks which was very imposing by the standards of the other huts in the neighbourhood.

Equally imposing, but in a different way, was Ama Kusunu. Those to whom Claudia had spoken in the village had directed them on their way with their lips curling downwards in an expression of distaste, even of disgust. It was as if they were speaking of an outcast.

The woman who opened the door of the house to them was a Métis elegantly dressed in a style that was totally out of keeping with the other inhabitants of the village.

For a moment Mrs. Quarshie and Claudia faced her in nonplussed silence and it was Ama herself who broke it. *"Vous désirez, mesdames?"* she asked and Claudia immediately took her up. She replied in rapid French saying, "We have been sent on a very delicate mission, madame. May we come in?"

The room into which Ama led them was furnished in a way which was familiar to both her visitors as being more or less European.

Though Ama's skin was dark her eyes were grey and her hair tawny red.

Claudia, realising that the onus of this interview lay on her, decided to take a chance and hope that news from Gambion had travelled less quickly than they had.

She said, "We come from Monsieur Akasaydoo."

The grey eyes were shrewd and distrusting. "You have something to prove that?"

Mrs. Quarshie, knowing that the piece of paper they had found in the raincoat would come into the conversation at some time, was holding it in her hand. Claudia took it from her and handed it to Ama who read, first, her own address and name.

"It is not enough," she said.

"The rest is on the other side," Claudia said, praying that was what Ama was waiting for. The half-caste turned the slip of paper over and looked at the hieroglyphics. After twisting the piece of paper back and forth in her hand several times she got up and left the room.

To Mrs. Quarshie's surprise Claudia crossed herself with the gesture normally used by Catholics and, as if in explanation, she whispered to Mrs. Quarshie, "It is the only juju I have with me, mama."

Mrs. Quarshie, who had more or less followed what was going on, said, "I hope it is a strong one."

Ama came back into the room carrying a large brown envelope.

She sat holding the envelope and said, "And now, mesdames, the money." And to Mrs. Quarshie in English, "You are Akhanian, no? P'rhaps you are Mrs. Quarshie and you will have the money, yes?"

"How do you know that?"

"That you are p'rhaps Mrs. Quarshie? It is, how you say, a good guess. I know your 'usband is on the Île de Sintra finding who kill Aka and why. He is clever man. Aka was a *salbête*. The money . . . if you are finding this piece of paper you are also finding the money. It is very simple, like one and one, you know. This paper is no good to me." She tapped the envelope. "Particularly when people will kill to get it. The money. That is different. With the money I can go back to where I like to be the most. Paris. She is my *ambiance*. Not this place of *femmes sauvages*. So if you give me the money you will 'ave the papers and we shall both be 'appy . . ."

Mrs. Quarshie thanked the prevision that had made her carry the money with her rather than banking it or hiding it in Claudia's hut.

She handed it over, apologising for the fact that it was very wet.

Ama smiled. "Hot money I am 'earing about. Dirty money also. Wet money is something new. But I can dry it and thank the *bon Dieu* that I do not 'ave to work for it this way any more."

*

It took the two women four hours to reach a fairly isolated frontier post between the Ebony Coast and Akhana. There Mrs. Quarshie told the Ebonese on duty that her bag and all her papers had been stolen in a nearby town. Fortunately she was with an Akhanian friend who could vouch for her. She was carrying a head-load of bolts of cloth for which she had a receipt.

Claudia handed over her passport for examination with a 500-franc CFA note folded inside it.

Within five minutes they were at the Akhanian post where Mrs. Quarshie unrolled one of the bolts of cloth and produced the passport which was supposed to have been stolen. Further inside the roll were the papers she had to deliver to Quarshie's uncle, the Permanent Secretary for Internal Affairs.

Having identified herself, she insisted on seeing the officer in charge of the post where she demanded action, and as her destination was the Ministry of Internal Affairs, the most powerful ministry in the country, she got it. She also demanded transport on state's business for Claudia to go to see Ajua Satay at the address they had been given by the bank manager—and she got that, too. Anyone seeing her use her authority the way she did would have realised that, given the need and the circumstances, she was just as formidable a person as her much more famous husband.

CHAPTER 16

Quarshie had not slept much.

The empty bed next to his was like an aching wound and there
was no form of local anaesthetic that could reduce the anxiety he
felt for his wife's safety. He was not torturing himself deliberately
when he worried about her; he was simply facing all the possi-
bilities as unemotionally as he could.

Jumbled with those painful considerations were others to which
he had to give his attention because whatever pattern of events
had his wife in control, there was nothing he could do about it.

Here on the Île de Sintra he had to try to anticipate the shape
of things to come, anticipate it and have a controlling hand in the
way it developed.

Because Antibonite was one element in the pattern, Quarshie
allowed his mind to turn over what he knew about voodoo.

African voodoo had had its beginning just across the border
from the village in which he had spent his childhood. It was a city
that reeked of history and of the occult. Kings and their priests had
lived there and followed their barbaric ways. Every hut and courtyard had its own iconographic memorials to Mawu-Lisa, Da, Fa
and other gods in the Fon hagiocracy. To Quarshie in his childhood and to the entire population of the town, these spirits, most
of them benign, occupied the highways and byways from sundown
to well beyond cock-crow. It was as if the city belonged to them
and they merely loaned it to humans during the daytime and re-
claimed it at night.

Now, though he could look back objectively at the trepidation that had filled him in the birthplace of voodoo, with its monuments where the mortar had been made with human blood and the sense it had given him of treading a fragile bridge over an abyss inhabited by spirits, though he could look back at such distant insecurities without queasiness, he still prepared to tackle the situation with wariness and caution.

A lot of events had to take place in the next two or three days if he was to come to any solutions of Akasaydoo's murder, and the first point that had to be cleared up was what role Antibonite was playing.

There was still almost an hour to go before dawn but Quarshie thought it was a good time to go for a walk to cleanse his mind of the night's restless images and to come to grips with the facts.

Outside the hotel the silence was only broken by the muted drum-roll beat of the diesel engines of a cargo ship steaming past the island on her way to sea. Again the water was calm. In the distance the lights of Gambion were no bigger than a scattering of gilded pin-heads stretching in a wide band across a sheet of black velvet.

For the moment everybody and everything seemed to be at rest except just the one ship and her crew and he, Quarshie, a lonely seeker in a jungle that was a tangle of parasitic and evil thorn bushes. Things were deceptively quiet at the moment. Even the sea seemed to be sleeping, though there had to be a suggestion of a breeze because he could smell the faint reek of diesel fumes from the cargo vessel.

Quarshie walked down to the harbour and sat on the wall at the end of the breakwater. In the distance there was already a faint stain of light growing slowly behind the land.

It was a good moment, he thought, to undertake an exercise which he had found useful. It was comparable to the old African necromancer's trick of throwing a handful of knuckle-bones, kola nuts, or beans on the ground and then, from the pattern in which they fell, divining the future.

In Quarshie's case he threw, metaphorically, all the facts, ideas and conclusions he had arrived at over his shoulder and then turned and faced them where they lay strewn behind him. It was a way of cleaning everything out of his system. Sometimes it led both to the discovery of something which had been lying concealed from sight under more recent concepts or information and to the bits and pieces falling into unexpected patterns.

Once again the device did not fail him. When he had assembled all the information he knew so far about Akasaydoo's murder, he turned his back on the predawn halo of light that was growing over the coast. Then he found he was facing the landing stage and that view triggered, immediately, a thought which had not occurred to him before.

It did not finalise anything but it raised a shade in one window so that for the first time he was able to get a glimpse of the inside of one of the rooms in the house which, to him, represented the structure of his case.

*

As he expected, Antibonite greeted him with a baleful expression. The prison cell in which he was incarcerated was very small. For furniture there was only a mat on the floor and now, for Quarshie, a chair that was carried in by one of the gendarmes.

For several moments the two men sat facing each other in silence until the guard came back again with two steaming mugs of black coffee.

Then Quarshie said, "I had the waiter in the hotel put a lot of sugar in your mug. It will make you feel better. Not as good as ganja, but a bit better. Drink it and then we'll talk." For a moment Quarshie thought that the Haitian was going to throw the hot liquid at him, but after a couple of seconds' hesitation he sipped and then drank the coffee slowly and some of his ill humour appeared to dissolve.

When he had finished he put the mug down, sucked the ends of his moustache and said, "So, man, what am I here for? What have I done?"

Quarshie shrugged. "Shall we say that it is something that would not make you very popular with Darapa if he knew about it?"

"I don't know what you're talking about."

"Last night after they took you and your woman to jail I went and searched your house. I am surprised at De Gobineau, or his wife, whichever of them it was who enrolled you, for not realising that you are not the right man for this job. You are playing in a game that is way out of your league. You know that?"

"I don't hear you, man. I know only one thing: as I and I come to reason with Rastafar I, I and I come to know the truth."

"Good, then we are on the same path."

"Then I and I welcome you, brother. But do you know that when you come to Rastafar you must give up the three revolutionary forces that is over the world and sanctified by Babylon and the Pope? They is politics, religion and commerce, the only three sins upon creation. Ain't no other sin. Comb, scissors, razor. De Rasta dreadlock wool ain't something artificial: comes from nature, I and I is born with it. De spirit of Selassie ain't something you can put on, man, like a winter coat. It mus' be planted deep like a seed. It's not something a dude can buy from no factory. It's there, man, inside him, and when a man destroys his hair, he destroys himself, the energy of Rasta I. He will na go forth and multiply. He dead, man . . . he dead already, already dead."

Quarshie humoured him. "You may be right, friend . . . that is the I and I part of you. Now let's talk to the other part. The part of you which works for the French who, aside from anything else, supply you with ganja. The weed is difficult to get here yet in your house you have enough to smoke twenty-four hours a day for months. But to me, my friend, you are hypocritical. You pretend to live the Rasta-way but use the rotten Babylon-way to support your habit. But there is something more than that, isn't there? De Gobineau can expose you as a ganja smoker, which is illegal here, but there is something else he has got on you, or you want out of him, isn't there? That's why you are working for him. Now, let me remind you of my position here. I'll be frank with you. My future depends on my being successful. If I don't solve the question of who killed Akasaydoo, everything, perhaps even my life, is at stake. Somebody has tried to kill me already. As a secret French agent here, if I hand you over to Darapa, you will die, and secretly, too, perhaps painfully. You see, you are careless. It's the ganja. It's what gives the French part of their hold on you and also makes you a poor operative. I suppose you were the only one they could get in here without tipping their hand to everyone."

"What did you find in my house?"

The mantle of Rastafarianism dropped from him.

Quarshie took a piece of paper out of his pocket.

Antibonite recognised it immediately.

He said, "Never trust a woman. I gave it to her to burn." Then with a hint of a smile he asked, "What does it tell you?"

Quarshie returned the smile. "Nothing. Only you and the woman who wrote it knows what it says. It's in code. But"—he put the letter to his nose—"Madame de Gobineau uses a very distinctive scent. It's probably the reason your woman kept it instead of destroying it. I visited the De Gobineau household and walked into the presence of this perfume like one walks into a mist."

Antibonite sank his head on his collar-bone so that his beard spread all over his chest and he stared at Quarshie. Presently he shrugged slightly and said, "OK, man. So what do you want from me?"

"Let's lay this whole thing out so that we both know where we stand. If Darapa knew you were tied up with the De Gobineaus it would be the chop for you, right? If I don't solve this little problem here it will mean the same thing for me. You co-operate with me and we may both get out alive."

"Even if I killed Akasaydoo?"

Quarshie smiled again and replied, "We'll talk about that later. For the moment I only want your help on one point. What had Akasaydoo got that everybody wanted?"

"Specifically, I don't know. It was a document and whatever it contained was straight poison to the French. The kind of thing that *Le Canard enchaîné* would love to get hold of because it might wreck the government. Some more hanky-panky that they have been up to out here no doubt. Man, it's one thing being a crook and something else again to be a cynical crook. I work for them because I hope one day I'll pick up something, like maybe what's in that document, which I can really screw them with, but good."

"You hate them so much? Even to the point of working for them in the hope that you will find a way to revenge yourself on them?"

"They is a plague, man. They is seducin' my people, makin' a mockery of them. Makin' a mockery of me. What've they got that I and I ain't got? Blood? Bone? Muscle? Brain? Yet they make like I and I is some kind of creature on a string, a creature they can yank this way and that. They took my people to Haiti and we rose up and drove them out of the island. It shall happen again, man. We shall drive them out of every land which don't belong to them even if we have to kill them all to do it. Like I said, I hate them and I don't need no other need to go after them—particularly to go after every Black like Akasaydoo who sells his soul to them by selling his people, *us,* you and I, and I and I."

CHAPTER 17

HISTORY   A famous African wizard used to proclaim that his course was "relentless," that his work involved killing and related to every act which was unlawful. He used to claim that the hyenas, the scavengers, were his grandchildren. However, he tried to excuse his malevolence by saying that most of those whom he killed "like beasts in the bush" brought their terrible deaths on themselves by being guilty of acts that were as merciless as those he committed.

When Quarshie got back to the hotel he found the manager sitting in the dusty, deserted foyer in a state of severe mental disturbance. He was a small man in late middle age with jowls, a broad flat nose, and hair which he wore close-cut on the side and back, forming a thick black pad on the top of his head.

The moment he saw Quarshie he leapt to his feet and came close to him before dragging four words out of his throat: "My brother is dead."

Nodding his head furiously he repeated, "Dead. He's dead."

"The Judge?"

Still nodding his head the man said, "He's dead."

"Where?"

The manager darted off up a wide staircase moving on his toes like a sprinter.

Quarshie mounted the steps more slowly behind him.

In front of the Judge's room the little man fumbled with a bunch of keys, found one that was evidently a master and threw open the door.

"*Là, mon Dieu.*"

Gesture and tone were theatrical.

"Come in and close the door. Lock it, we don't want to be disturbed," Quarshie told his companion and walked towards the bed where the old man was lying.

Quarshie raised one of the Judge's eyelids and felt the temperature of the side of his neck with the back of his hand.

When he turned to the manager he was sitting bent forward in a chair with his elbows on his knees and his face behind clenched fists.

Gently the Doctor said, "You are right, he is dead and has been for quite a long time. Who found him and who else knows about this?"

With an effort the manager replied, "I found him. I came up to see why he had not come to breakfast. He likes his coffee very hot and his croissant warm. They were both getting cold." He looked up at Quarshie with his mouth open as if he were going to cry but no sound came. With difficulty he swallowed and said, "He was a good man, a very good man. Find me the murderer, Doctor, and I will kill him."

"We don't know yet, my friend, that he was murdered. I will first have to examine him and the room. You had better stay with me while I do those things. I'm sorry, very sorry. You are right, he was a good man and if he was murdered I will find the man who did it, you understand? But first, no one must know about this, not for a while at least. You will keep silent?"

The manager nodded his head miserably. "If it will help, Doctor. If it will help." And dropped his face back in his hands.

Quarshie felt pity for the man and then anger against the man who had brought about the Judge's death. It was a strong, ugly feeling and for several moments he enjoyed it and made no effort to repress it. Then he pushed it aside and started examining the body as coolly as if the old man had been a stranger killed in a street accident.

The Judge was dressed for bed in the African fashion, with a cloth wound around his waist covering his legs down to his shins. There was no trace of injury or wounds on his head or torso. When Quarshie loosed the roll of cloth at the top of the Judge's nightwear to examine the lower part of his body he found an envelope, with his name on it, folded into the cloth. Almost guiltily he slipped it into the pocket of his jacket so that the Judge's brother would not see it. Then he completed his examination, certain now that he would not find any injuries.

All the time the manager sat quite still, lost in his unhappiness. Quarshie looked slowly around the room trying to determine where he should start his search and at the same time looking for somewhere he could read the letter he had in his pocket.

The room was sparsely furnished. There was nothing but the essentials: bed, side-table, wardrobe, two chairs, a chest of drawers and a bedside lamp. In one corner there was a door into a toilet and shower. Quarshie headed for it and closed the door behind him.

Quickly he took the envelope out of his pocket, slit it open and glanced over the single page of handwritten text.

Forgive me, old friend, for what I am about to do.
When they tried to kill you yesterday I knew that this
terrible farce had gone too far. I have been under great
pressure that you should be steered away from other investigations, hence that charade in the barracoon with
the vevé being drawn on my back. Quarshie, it has become too much for me. At least my family are safe now.
Friends helped them to get away a few days ago. Now I
am responsible only for myself and for you. Ponongo is
your man. He is very dangerous. Be careful. Forgive me
my duplicity. Kwamé

Without reading it again Quarshie put the letter away and see-ing a sponge bag on the top of the cistern behind the toilet he opened it and found, instantly, the item he had been expecting to find. It was a bottle labelled Luminal 60 and it was empty. Pheno-barbitone, in a very strong dose. The size of the bottle suggested that it could have contained 200 to 250 tablets, enough to kill half a dozen people or more, let alone one old man.

Again Quarshie raged inside himself.

When so much pressure is put on a man that he is forced to commit suicide, his death becomes murder.

If he worked only with the information that he had available to him, he wondered, how could he ensure that justice would be done?

Dictators and their minions in their own countries are above the law, or protected from it by corruption, he thought. So his ques-tion seemed to be unanswerable. Certainly it needed more consid-eration.

He went back into the bedroom where the manager was now standing at the window looking out towards Gambion. When he heard Quarshie open and close the door to the bathroom he turned and the Doctor saw that he had been crying.

However, his voice was more controlled than it had been. *"Eh bien, m'sieu.* You have found something? How did my brother die?"

"By taking an overdose of barbiturates. That is what I believe. A post-mortem will have to be made to prove what can be no more than a supposition until that is done. However, it is good enough for me to be convinced that I am right and . . . and, for reasons I will explain later, his death and how it came about must be kept to ourselves until I can think about what action I should take next. *Entendu?"*

"Kwamé thought very highly of you, Doctor. If he were here he would tell me to do exactly what you say and to ask no questions. It is what I shall do. Is there anything else?"

Quarshie nodded. "Help me carry him to my room. There, there is a bath. We will fill it with cold water and you will, as secretly as you can, bring me ice. We must keep his body as cold as we can for a day or two. I shall see that my door and the bathroom door are locked, and you, personally, must bring me ice whenever you can. Yes?"

"Yes, m'sieu. What are you going to do?"

"I am not sure yet. I must think about it carefully. The question goes beyond the law, you understand?"

"You mean he was killed?"

"Certainly, and by a man whose only reason for seeing him dead was because he refused, in the end, to betray his belief in honesty and loyalty to his friends." He bent over the old man's body putting his arms underneath him. "I will carry him. You open both doors and see that the corridor is clear."

*

In his room, alone except for the dead man in the bath, Quarshie questioned his reasons for taking the action that had been inspired by instinct.

Ponongo had been the prime suspect in the murder of Akasaydoo for some time. He had been puzzled, however, by his seemingly airtight alibi. He had been seen leaving the island the day before Akasaydoo had been killed and he had returned the day after the event.

That alibi, however, had been the subject of Quarshie's closure when he had been on the pier early in the morning and remembered the report that three Arabs and a couple of their women had disembarked on the day of the murder and re-embarked the following morning. It would have been easy for the light-skinned Ponongo to stick a moustache and goatee beard on his face and wear a pair of dark glasses. To a casual observer there would have been no suggestion that one of the Arabs was in fact Ponongo.

Also Yasin had seen him asleep in his room fully clothed the morning after the Judge had been subjected to the inscription of the vevé on his back. Then there had been the dispatch of the GES men to reinforce the brigadier's contingent on the island where they would be on hand to take orders from the one GES executive left there, Ponongo. Perhaps the attempt on his own life had been meant to fail. Perhaps the man had been meant to miss and only frighten him to make sure that he kept in line. There was the fact that Ponongo had served in Brazil where the curare he had used to kill the guards outside the barracoon would have been available and he could easily have come in contact with expatriate Africans who practiced macumba and knew about vevés. Finally, he had a telephone in his house and could have used it to call Quarshie to the barracoon on the night of the assault of the Judge.

Now his suspicions had been confirmed by the Judge's note.

Ponongo was the man and behind him stood Darapa.

At the moment neither of them would be likely to guess that Quarshie was so close to them, but how could he arrange for justice to be done? His thoughts had brought him full circle back to that question. The answer would not be simple.

*

As Quarshie was debating his next move, the regular daily air service from Port Saint Mary, in Akhana, landed at Gambion. The captain, a fat jovial man with a thick black moustache, handing over various types of manifest to the Akhana Airways representative at the airport, told him, after looking around to see that no one else was in earshot, "There's a 'most urgent' in here." He nodded to the papers he held in his hand. "From the Ministry of Internal Affairs. It was handed to me by a special messenger and I was told to tell you it has to get to the embassy 'at once,' repeat 'at once,' or somebody would be getting a rocket up his right trouser leg. OK?"

"OK, Captain."

"But you are not to arouse anyone's interest or suspicions about it."

"Yes sir."

It was not the first time "most urgent" messages had been passed between the Akhana government and their representatives in this way. It was common knowledge that the telephone and telex lines connecting all institutions in the Ebony Coast with outside authorities were tapped.

The message was carried, therefore, by a boy on a bicycle, the same one who normally carried bills of lading and other similar documents between the airport and the Akhana Airways town office. He was sent on with it from the airline office to the embassy where the first councillor discovered that the outer envelope contained another envelope, addressed to Dr. Quarshie. He was a resourceful man who realised that whatever the letter contained had to be kept out of the hands of anyone save the addressee, so he arranged, through a friend on the dockside, to meet the captain of the Île de Sintra ferry in a café on the other side of the town. He gave the captain the letter and told him that he must personally deliver it to Quarshie and that if he returned with a signed receipt from the Doctor which stated that he had received it with the seals unbroken, the man would receive the equivalent of two weeks' wages. A quarter of that sum being delivered, on account, at once.

In due course that evening, the captain returned with the receipt and was paid the rest of the money.

CHAPTER 18

HISTORY In native African law it is seldom possible for a man to be presented before a court and, after a brief hearing, judged and sentenced, because there are very few statutory penalties. There is nothing automatic or mechanical about African law and each seeming malefaction has to be assessed in relation to all related circumstances and in the light of all the evidence. Nothing can be regarded, from the outset, as cut and dried because the court's concern is related to justice rather than what is right in law.

Quarshie telephoned the President. Knowing that his call would probably be monitored by Madame de Gobineau he was at first circumspect in what he said when Darapa came on the line. He told the President that he had vital information to communicate. He also told him of the attempt that had been made on his life.

"Did you get the man who came after you?"

"I did."

"The police have him?"

"I killed him."

For a moment there was silence at the other end of the line. It was followed by a short laugh and the comment, "What a formidable man you are, Doctor."

"Whoever was responsible for setting up the attempt could well try again," Quarshie continued. "I would rather speak with you before that happens but I don't like to leave the island because I am expecting important information to come through at any moment."

"But you have something to show me?"

"Someone." And with sudden delight at the consternation he might cause to the De Gobineaus, Quarshie added, "I have a Haitian in police custody. The information he can give will be of interest to you. I also have someone else you should talk to. It would be best if we could have our meeting as late this evening as possible."

"Why?"

"By then I should have the papers you are so anxious to see."

"Ah. They won't be available before then?"

"No."

"Then I will come. Please arrange with Ponongo to be ready to receive me."

The President rang off. It had been too easy, Quarshie thought. Then he wondered if he was being foolhardy.

Soon he knew that this suspicion was correct, for within an hour, the brigadier came to his door to tell him that Anton Antibonite was dead and one of the gendarmes, who had been seconded to his command, was missing. The Haitian had been shot through the head while sitting on the floor of his cell.

"Why?" asked the brigadier. "Why?"

Quarshie closed his eyes and thought of the "delight" he had felt at the consternation the information he had given the President would stir up in the De Gobineaus.

"How did the gendarme get away?" he asked irritably. "And do you know anything about him?"

"He did not get away. He belonged to the GES and I will find him. But why kill Antibonite?"

"He was working for the French and . . . I suppose they heard that we had picked him up," Quarshie replied, hating himself. He shook his head and the brigadier, putting his own interpretation on the Doctor's gesture, said, "Yes, m'sieu. It is wrong. We live in a rotten world."

"With rotten people in it," Quarshie added, turning the knife in his own gut. "Well, find the killer. But first I have to tell you that this evening we shall be having a visit from the President and I want to make arrangements for his reception. Here is what I propose . . ."

After listening to Quarshie's plan the brigadier went away surprised and thoughtful while Quarshie, after the blunder he had made over Antibonite, wondered how he had the nerve to continue with a project that was certainly going to put at risk many more lives.

*

Much later, as he stood on the sand outside the barracoon with the moon throwing zigzags of light on the sea and the waves pawing gently at the beach, he became involved in another period of anxiety about his plan. It involved four other people and to a large extent depended on whether he had been right to put his trust in them.

He looked anxiously at the guard who was standing out of the moonlight near the entry port. Had he made wise choices in those whom he had called upon to help him? Might they, too, end up dead like Antibonite? And would those he intended to surprise react in the way it seemed reasonable to expect they would? How about his own nerves? There was a point in the exercise at which he was most likely to have to take chances with his own life. Was he prepared to do that simply to find and punish the murderer? Since there was no way he was going to trust the Ebonese forces of law and order, he would have to be the judge and executioner. So, was he prepared to lay his life on the line and to pass judgement on another man in pursuit of some kind of justice?

Then he jeered at himself and his introspection. This was the last round. The gong had already sounded. In fact, he had sounded it himself. Now he was in the ring and his only option was to fight. He was used to winning and would win again.

The steaming-lights of a ship caught his eye, a lower light in front, a higher light behind it. Below them both a red light and the dimmer blur of deck lights and one or two portholes showing lights burning in cabins. Nothing very dramatic going on there, he thought. The ship was moving slowly. Gradually she came to a stop. Then there was a sudden rasp of sound as an anchor was dropped and the chain raced through the hawse.

The masthead lights and the red port light went out and a riding light blinked into existence over the fo'c'sle, followed shortly by the lights being switched off in the wheel-house and on the bridge. Bed, Quarshie thought, bunks for everyone except an anchor watch. While here, we wait. So he had not shaken off his nerves. Then he would have to live with them. He was just on his way over to have a word with the guard when he saw the men he was expecting walking along the beach towards him.

There were six of them. The President, Ponongo, three guards all carrying guns, and the brigadier. So far so good. He had reckoned on up to six guards.

He walked towards them with the sand clogging his footsteps, making them laboured.

Darapa appeared to be in a good humour, laughing and talking to Ponongo. "Well, Doctor," he called as they approached each other, "what kind of gala are you going to stage for us tonight?"

Quarshie was unprepared for his geniality and could not answer it in kind knowing that someone's death, maybe his own, could well be part of the spectacle.

"I believe you should find it interesting," he replied.

"Good, good. And was the delivery you were expecting made?"

"It was not a matter of delivering the item, but of finding it."

"And you did find it?"

"Yes."

Quarshie looked covertly at Ponongo. The younger man was not carrying himself in his usual relaxed and elegant manner. Quarshie wondered whether an official executioner ever felt any pity for a condemned man as he stood on the drop under the gallows. Was it possible to feel pity for a man who killed in cold blood? And what about executioners? Didn't they kill in cold blood, too? Of course, but the authority and therefore the responsibility lay with someone else. Here he was operating on his own authority and was therefore fully responsible for anything that happened.

Darapa was saying, "The brigadier told me about the Haitian. If you can trace anything directly to the De Gobineaus, let me know. Don't initiate any action yourself. My relationship with them is very tricky. A lot of money that their government pays into our finances has to be endorsed by De Gobineau. It is an . . . ah . . . an unsatisfactory situation but one I have to live with. You understand?"

"Yes sir."

"Now these papers Akasaydoo had picked up. They are of extreme importance, as you must know, because—I am sure you must have read them?" He was probing.

"I have not had them long enough. They are in code."

Darapa gave Quarshie a sharp look.

"Then how do you know they are the right ones?"

"Only because they were valuable enough for someone to kill for them."

"And get them?"

"No. They were under the murderer's nose and he did not see them because he did not look in the right place."

Again Quarshie glanced at Ponongo. The younger man's expression looked as if it had been cast in cement.

The President stopped outside the entrance to the barracoon

and put his hand on Quarshie's arm. "And tell me, Doctor, why did you send Mrs. Quarshie back to Akhana—because that is where she is, isn't it? My people lost track of her." He sounded plaintive. "Someone attacks you and you don't just arrest him. You kill him. Someone follows your wife to see that she is not getting into mischief dashing off into the bush and she breaks his ankle."

It was news to Quarshie.

He said, "I sent her away because she was a liability. She increased my vulnerability to attack, as you well know, sir. You used her as a hostage yourself."

In a curious way they respected each other, circling each other all the time, looking for an opening to throw in a damaging punch.

"And that was the only reason?"

"Isn't it enough? I have a son. I don't want him to be left an orphan."

"A praiseworthy attitude . . . and yet, I still wonder if there was not some other motive. You see, I am not a very trusting man. Ah, well . . ." The President shrugged and added in an offhand way, "Running a country is not an easy task. It makes me wish that I could count on people like you being on my side. Now let's go and see what new surprises you have in store for me."

Strange little man, Quarshie thought as the President preceded him along the tunnel into the barracoon, strange and unpredictable.

A judgement which Darapa justified a moment later as he came into the courtyard of the barracoon and saw Yasin stretched out on the flogging block. She was dressed in a sacrificial white *panja* with the cloth wound around her body under her armpits and stretching to below her knees. Her hands and feet were secured to the rings set into the stone slab on which she lay.

Darapa's reaction was no more violent than it would have been if he had entered a museum to look at a display of mummified human or animal remains.

A kerosene pressure-lamp had been set on a bench near the flogging block. Darapa walked over to and slowly around the young woman, inspecting her from every angle. Finally he turned to Quarshie. "And who do we have here?" he asked.

"Her name is Yasin Barafat. She was a friend of Akasaydoo's—though perhaps friend is not the right word. She wanted to kill him as he had killed her father. She may have been the associate of whomever it was who did, eventually, put an end to his life. However, Akasaydoo certainly never thought of her as an enemy. Indeed, she must have been very close to him, because it was to her that he gave the task of concealing the papers which you have been looking for."

"I see. But isn't this a rather melodramatic way of conveying that information to me? Could you not have presented her to me in the normal manner?"

"Yes sir. However, the person I wanted to impress by this little drama was Monsieur Ponongo. I thought perhaps he might like to deal with Mademoiselle Barafat in the same way that he dealt with the man Akasaydoo . . . by cutting her throat while she is lying helpless on the block."

As he spoke, Quarshie raised his hand in a signal and the two guards who had been on duty outside the barracoon and had accompanied the party into it, moved along with the brigadier, to places immediately behind each of the guards who had been accompanying the President and Ponongo. Unnoticed, they had earlier closed and bolted the massive doors of the barracoon behind the party as it had entered. They now held their rifles menacingly pointing at the backs of the other three men in uniform.

Addressing the latter, Quarshie said, "Drop your guns. Those who stand behind you have no love for any of you, or for any other member of the GES."

The men reacted slowly and Adedeni, who was one of the two men who had been on guard (the other was Sharp), was inclined to be impatient and jabbed the barrel of his rifle hard against the spine of the man in front of him. The man squawked in surprise and pain and dropped his gun. The others followed his example.

"Now, sir." Quarshie turned to Darapa. "Since Mademoiselle Barafat has done her job, which was to bait the trap and give my helpers time to bolt the doors and move into the positions they are in now, I will release her. In the meantime, please stand quite still, both of you." He included the President and Ponongo in his gesture. "And, brigadier, take these men away and put them in one of the cells where once slaves were kept. Post one man here and one man to guard the prisoners."

Quarshie removed the bonds from Yasin and helped her off the flogging block.

Darapa, still apparently unflustered, said, "Very neat, Doctor. However, I don't need to warn you not to do anything foolish. I brought many more men on the boat with me. If anything should happen to me, or should you keep me here for an unreasonable length of time, you will never leave the island alive."

"Like your old friend and my old friend the Judge."

"Why, what happened to him?" The tone of surprise in Darapa's voice sounded genuine.

"You drove him to suicide."

For a fraction of a moment Darapa's urbane expression fell to pieces. Then, with a determined effort, he recovered his composure.

"I heard nothing about that. You are right. He was an old friend. We stood together, side by side, to face De Gaulle in the days of the *Rassemblement Démocratique*. I am sorry. We are, were, the same age but we had different ambitions." He shrugged slightly. "I didn't think he would give in that way or that easily." He paused. "So, Doctor? Are we, he and I, to stand together again . . . this time to face God? Is that your plan, even though, I repeat, it would mean you would be joining us?"

Quarshie shook his head. "When you do go to stand before any final arbiter, sir, it will take one as all-knowing and all-powerful as He to pass judgement on you. I can only judge those like this young man here, who deceive and kill for small, mean prizes."

Ponongo came to life. Suddenly he had a revolver in his hand. Quarshie turned to Yasin, who was standing beside him and said, "Go and stand with Adé." Then he turned back to Ponongo and pointed at the gun he was holding. "What are you going to do with that?"

"Kill you."

"That means, of course, that you admit the charges I made against you and that you, too, will die, because these other men have orders to prevent you from getting away alive."

"Then they also will be killed by the men *Monsieur le Président* brought with him."

"I am not sure that they will. You see, *Monsieur le Président* does not know, as I do, that like Akasaydoo you were serving two masters, the De Gobineaus and the Monsieur here. Also that you were prepared to extort money from them just as your victim, Akasaydoo, did. You killed him and took over his plan."

"You are making that up. You have no proof."

"I have proof." Turning to Darapa, Quarshie started to say, *"Monsieur le Président,* your man here was . . ."

Ponongo fired.

For the first time that night Quarshie felt a sense of relief. The risks he had taken were paying off.

He walked towards Ponongo to take the gun away from him and the young man fired again at point-blank range.

Quarshie said, "You are a murderous, vicious, traitorous scoundrel like the man you slaughtered here. You caused the Judge to take his own life and now you are trying to kill me."

The third time Ponongo pulled the trigger the explosion from the gun blackened the front of the Doctor's shirt and Quarshie took his would-be assailant by the left wrist and pulled him into a short arm jab with his right fist, which bent the half-caste double. Quarshie's next blow, a chopping rabbit punch to the back of Ponongo's neck, was lethal. He dropped to the ground at Quarshie's feet, lifeless.

The Doctor broke the long silence which followed by turning to the brigadier. "Did you get the man who killed Antibonite?" he asked.

"Yes, m'sieu. He had nowhere to go and we knew him because he received a telephone call from the mainland just a few minutes before the murder. Like most GES men all he knew how to do was to follow orders."

"The call was doubtless from the De Gobineaus but they will deny it. And, as *Monsieur le Président* here says, they have more than diplomatic immunity. Do you have nothing to say, sir?" Quarshie turned to the President.

Darapa looked grey, but his response to Quarshie's question was cool enough.

"Yes, Doctor, I have something to say. That business with the pistol was a neat trick. Are you wearing some kind of a bullet-proof vest?"

"No. I knew Ponongo had the gun because he threatened me with it when he forced the Judge to play that dramatic game with me right here. This young lady"—he indicated Yasin—"found it for me. She borrowed it and the brigadier replaced the live ammunition in it with blank cartridges."

"You took a chance, didn't you, that he would not notice the substitution?"

"The chambers of that gun are short, sir. Even in this light I could see that they were not fully charged. That is, that there were no bullets in it, only cartridges. If it had been fully armed the brigadier was ready, at a glance from me, to shoot first."

"I see. Ingenious. So may we now proceed to the question of the documents. After all this . . . this melodrama, I suppose you will still honour your contract? I suppose you do have the documents?"

"Of course, I have them."

"And I have you. You cannot leave this country or this island without my permission."

"You make it sound too simple, sir. There is an important decision that you have to make first. You see, we, my wife and I, have the documents, I received confirmation of that fact earlier this evening, but they are not here and you are going to have to decide whether they are more valuable to you than my life and the lives of my friends who helped me in this, as you called it, melodrama."

Darapa closed his eyes and the muscles of his lean jaws worked as if he were chewing on a very tough piece of meat.

Into the silence Quarshie injected one more short sentence. "You see, sir," he said, "I am not a very trusting man, either."

CHAPTER 19

"I beat him, yet he won. Why?"

Quarshie said, "If ancestors there be they will judge Ponongo and they will judge me for killing him."

The Doctor was back in Akhana with Mrs. Quarshie and his uncle, the Permanent Secretary, sitting in the latter's office with several bottles of beer on the table beside him.

The old man said, "You deliberately provoked Ponongo. You knew the way he would react. You wanted to kill him."

Quarshie said, "Somebody had to stop him. In my short experience of him he had killed Akasaydoo, two guards, indirectly the Judge, and he was trying to kill me."

Mrs. Quarshie shook her head. "That business with the revolver must have been as close as I have ever come to being a widow."

Quarshie let the observation pass. "What exactly was in those all-important papers?" he asked his uncle. "I presume you read them?"

"I made a copy of them. It is in this file. I guessed you were going to need the original for an instant trade. Though I was surprised to see Darapa on the plane with you."

Quarshie smiled. "He and I are in complete agreement about one thing. We can't trust each other. You haven't answered my question."

"It is hot stuff. Worth a lot of hush money from the French government. Eyewitness accounts from six men who saw French paratroopers snatch three American geologists, who were working on their own, up in the Valley of the Serpent. So far as the world was concerned the French were using helicopters to fly in aid to the starving. They must have heard of the corundum find, which might lead to other more important geological discoveries. My investigations suggest that both sides, the geologists and the French, agreed to a cover-up and to joint plans to exploit the discoveries."

"I wonder how much misery has been caused in the world by the implications of that word 'exploit.'" Quarshie turned to his wife. "And Ajua Satay?"

"She wouldn't talk. One draws one's own conclusions. She certainly came home with a lot of money. Enough to buy herself a car. She's the only person in the neighbourhood to buy a *new* one for years."

"Let me see," said the Permanent Secretary. He looked down at a pad on his knee on which, in his best bureaucrat's manner, he had made some notes. "There are one or two questions you have not answered. For instance, what was actually going on between the Judge and Ponongo?"

"The GES had been persecuting the old man for a long time. He had always refused to toe the line and was regarded as an enemy, and Ponongo saw an opportunity to turn up the heat again. As the Judge told me, they always did that in the same way, by threatening to harm his family. The whole motivation behind Ponongo's killing Akasaydoo was so that he could get hold of these papers." Quarshie tapped the file the Permanent Secretary had given him. "With them he could have asked any price he liked from Darapa and the French, just as Akasaydoo had, but with my being there and my close friendship with the Judge, things weren't moving smoothly enough or quickly enough for him. So he forced the Judge, with the usual threats, to play his part in that obscene little charade in the barracoon. He relied on the Judge's fear of reprisals against his family to keep his mouth shut about the games our nasty friend was playing. Ultimately, the poor old man, who I am sure hated deceiving me, as well as others, could put up with it no more. Once his family was safely out of the way he killed himself."

"And the drawing of the vevé on the block under Akasaydoo?"

"Ponongo again, of course. It had to be. He was trying to lay a false trail to Antibonite and through him to the French because he knew that Antibonite was working for them. Then, I think, it occurred to him that Antibonite knew too much about vevés and might identify the thing on the block as having Bahian origins—vodu is strong in Bahia, almost as strong as it is in Haiti—and that might lead me to the conclusion I had come to already, that it had been carried out by someone with South American connections. Of course, Ponongo had already set that train of thought working when he used curare to kill the guards and it might have set up that line of thought earlier, if I had been on the ball, when I learned that tubocurarine had been used in Akasaydoo's murder. I was a bit slow."

Mrs. Quarshie was not sure whether she wanted to kiss her large husband or slap him. She decided on the former because she knew him well enough to be sure that his modesty was genuine and not false.

The Permanent Secretary consulted his notes again. "Finally, what about Adé, Sharp and Yasin?" he asked.

"Once I knew that the murderer was Ponongo it obviously meant that, in one way or another, they were on my side. Adé and Ponongo had also had a falling out at the bar in the hotel one night. I learned that from the barman just before I left. They hated each other. That stupid note I got about Adé had Ponongo's nasty little mind written all over it. And of course there was no problem in persuading Sharp where his duty lay."

"And Yasin?" Mrs. Quarshie asked.

"She thinks I am very handsome."

"Samuel Quarshie . . ." The tone of Mrs. Quarshie's voice was faintly threatening.

The Doctor grinned. "Well, let's just say that she, too, was very willing to co-operate. She could see that Ponongo had the same disease that had infected Akasaydoo." He stood up. To the Permanent Secretary he said, "Thanks for the beer, Uncle, and all the help you have given with these documents." And to his wife he said, "We'd better go and see how they have been getting on at the clinic."

"I was at the clinic yesterday. I think we should go home."

"We will . . . later."

*

It was, in fact, quite a bit later, and Mrs. Quarshie was lying in bed with her head on Quarshie's shoulder. Presently she said, "Without looking up I can tell you haven't even got your eyes shut. What's the matter?"

Quarshie sighed and answered, "The world, the flesh and the devil. The only Presidents we get in West Africa who make a name for themselves are those who can hold on to power. That seems to be the yardstick by which their success is measured. The people in the villages, the vast majority of the population, are helpless. They have no power to influence what happens in gov-

ernment, therefore they have no power to influence the selection
of a President.

"When the Whites left we thought we were going to create a
great future. What we have now is what we have made of it and
it's not much. When they were here we were self-sufficient in food.
Now we have to import even palm and ground-nut oil and part of
what we should be spending on the food goes to import cars and
appliances for the rich. The big towns are overcrowded and a
mess. We have more schools but all they produce are young people for whom there is no work and financially we have become
beggars. It's not all our own fault but an awful lot of it is.

"Above all we are ruled by Darapas—men who accept that the
system is corrupt and use the power that gives them mostly for
their own ends. That little monkey-man I have been dealing with
has more blood on his hands than a busy potter has wet clay. But
what could I do? Nothing. I beat him, yet he won. Why? Why are
we so powerless?"

Mrs. Quarshie stared absent-mindedly at a big, flying beetle that
was trying to smash its way into the light bulb on the lamp beside
the bed. Eventually she asked, "Do you think you are the only
person in West Africa who feels the way you do?"

"No. I am sure there are many others."

"Then, my man, there is still hope. Arimi is showing that he is
inheriting your heart. So, some men who are honest and can reason clearly will always be there. You and Arimi and others like
you both may not yet see the path through the forest because the
bush is thick and has been growing for a long time. But one day
you will. You, or those who follow you, and that, for me, is
knowledge enough."

Quarshie tightened his arm around his wife's shoulder but he
said nothing, not wishing to involve her any further in the turmoil
which filled his mind.

About the Author

John Wyllie is the author of eight previous novels featuring the resourceful Dr. Quarshie, including *A Tiger in Red Weather, The Killer Breath, A Pocket Full of Dead,* and *Death Is a Drum . . . Beating Forever.* The author is a Canadian who flew with the RAF in World War II. He has spent many years in West Africa and now lives in Ireland.